KITTEN CABOODLE

CANDACE HARPER

A CLOVER HILL ROMANCE

contents

about this book

Daphne wants three things: to build her solo business as a wedding planner, stay in her home without breaking the bank, and figure out the next steps in her life. Taking a housemate will help with at least one of those.

Enter Cade, golden retriever gym bro who needs a place to stay in Clover Hill while he helps to open a new chiropractor's clinic. He doesn't mind being far from home, and he might be the answer to all of Daphne's problems.

Neither of them are looking for romance, but when an instant attraction sparks between them, who are they to turn away?

Fate, friends and a cat bring them together, but is it enough to keep Cade in Clover Hill?

Kitten Caboodle is a medium heat, low angst trans m / cis f small town contemporary romance novella. It takes place in the shared world of Clover Hill, so it can be read as part of the series or as a standalone.

❃

content warnings

Heat Level: High heat (frequent references to sexual arousal and attraction, multiple brief sexually arousing encounters, one long graphic sex scene)

- Not super explicit sex scenes, masturbation scenes
- Alcohol usage
- Cursing
- Discussion of job insecurity, housing insecurity
- Lost/missing cat
- Worry over an animal's health (always fine, though!)
- Minor injury caused by cat (everybody's fine! Cats are just sharp sometimes)
- Accidental (cat) pregnancy
- Graphic details of animal birth
- Discussion of fat and trans bodies

one

. . .

Cade waved his final patient of the day out the door with a tired smile on his face. It had been a long day, but a good one.

Two people had graduated from their physical therapy programs and he had gotten to see his favorite patient. Mrs. Fleinhardt was an eighty-five-year-old woman he had been working with for a few months after her hip replacement. She always attempted to set him up with whichever one of her grandkids had accompanied her. Tonight, though, she'd been too tired to do much more than introduce them.

The sound of the door closing behind her seemed to summon his boss. Dr. Daniel Schwartz poked his head around the corner and brightened when he saw Cade was alone. "Do you have a few minutes to talk before you go? I've got an idea I want to run by you."

Cade had to hold back a sigh. He'd wanted to go home and take a shower, but something about Doc's expression made Cade think this was something more serious than the simple words were letting on. "Sure. I'll come back to your office when I'm done closing out today's appointments for billing." Normally, the receptionist took care of this, but they'd had to leave early to take care of a sick kid.

"Don't take too long. This is important." Doc said, sending a shiver down Cade's spine.

Cade nodded, and Doc disappeared back around the corner that led to the one truly closed-off space in the building. The words did not help him focus on the work in front of him, and he felt his guts twisting with worry.

It was rare for the older man to be serious, and it was even rarer for him to be secretive about literally anything. The man hadn't even been able to keep last year's 'surprise' bonuses a secret for longer than a week, for Pete's sake.

But eventually, Cade finished the paperwork, leaving it for the receptionist to double-check in the morning, and went to the office, knocking gently.

He half expected to find his boss sitting in a large wingback chair, turning like he was a movie villain who'd been expecting him.

But that was silly. The man was a chiropractor—he didn't even have a proper chair. Almost every time Doc had to work at his desk, he sat on a yoga ball.

"Come in, Cade." Doc's gravelly voice was cheerful, and Cade pushed open the door. Sure enough, there was his boss, bouncing away like a kid at a playground. The normality of the motion went a long way to soothe his worry.

"Have a seat, son. I'm sure your feet hurt after being on them all day. And there's no need to look so worried. Everything's just fine. In fact, I have a proposition for you."

Cade froze halfway into the plush armchair usually

reserved for patients and stared at his boss. "A proposition?"

"Yes, a proposition. You remember meeting my son Bryan at last year's Chanukah party, right?"

Cade blinked at the seeming non-sequitur while he thought back to the previous December, trying to remember which one of Doc's sons was Bryan. All three of the Schwartz kids had been at the party, to their parents' delight. If Cade remembered correctly, Bryan was the one who had brought his partner home for the first time.

Cade hadn't immediately recognized Bryan as a Schwartz because he looked almost nothing like his father. Where Doc and the other two were short, stocky, and in various stages of balding, Bryan was tall, lanky, and had a head full of blond curls like his mother. And his partner, Kavanaugh, had worn a suit tailored so sharply Cade had been surprised it didn't cut anyone who looked at them wrong.

Cade had gotten along with them both and even bonded with Kavanaugh a little in transmasc solidarity. He always loved meeting more trans people, even if they lived pretty far away and he was unlikely to see them often.

"Good, I'm glad you remember him. You probably recall he's the only one of my sons who chose to go into this fine profession, and I must say, he's proven to be quite excellent at it. Now he's finished his doctorate and gotten his license, and he wants to open his own practice in the town he and his partner live in."

"Good for him!" Cade had no idea why this required a one-on-one talk, but Doc was obviously proud, and Cade was happy for him. "Starting a practice sounds exciting."

Doc puffed out his chest with fatherly satisfaction. "I'm glad to hear you say that."

Now Cade was back to being confused. "Sir?"

"You've been my office manager in addition to doing PT for how many years now?"

"Three?"

"And how many times has there been a problem you didn't know how to handle?"

Cade had to think. "I mean, maybe twice? We have solid policies." He should know. He'd written or updated most of them himself.

"Exactly. Bryan's a fantastic chiropractor, but he doesn't know how to start a practice from the ground up. He doesn't know how to run an office. You know all of that stuff. You run this place like a well-adjusted spine." Doc laughed so hard at his own joke that he snorted.

Cade was still mystified as to where this conversation was going, but if his boss was cracking bad jokes and throwing out compliments, he couldn't be in any real trouble. "Well, I'm sure he'll hire someone with the experience to help him get started. Plus, you'll only be a phone call away if he has any questions, right?"

"I will. But, it's funny you mentioned hiring someone. That's actually what I wanted to talk to you about. He's going to need help, and I think you two would make a powerful team."

Doc looked at him expectantly, but Cade had no idea what he was looking for. After a few seconds, Cade spoke hesitantly. "I'd be happy to talk him through some of the basics, certainly. We can hop on a video call any time."

"Actually, I was thinking about something a little more hands-on. If you'd be amenable, I'd like to pay for you to move there temporarily and help him get his business set up."

Say what now? Every fleeting thought in Cade's brain came to a screeching halt.

The shock must have shown on his face, because Doc raised his hands in a 'wait' gesture and began speaking again. "Let me clarify, not a permanent move. I was thinking three months would be long enough for you to help him get him started, connect with the community as a businessman and hire and train his staff."

The idea was shocking—and would be a huge responsibility—but it also sounded kind of great. He'd need to make arrangements for his fish and plants before he went, and... "Hold on, could you go without me for that long? I've never been gone longer than a week since I became a manager."

Doc laughed a little. "We'd need to hire another physical therapist for sure, but I think between the two of us, Andrew and I would be able to handle most of your managerial duties."

Right. Of course they could.

"Well, I would want to talk to Bryan about some specifics and we'd have to figure out somewhere for me to stay, but that sounds like it could be a lot of fun. If it's not too much trouble for you, I'd like to give it a shot. What's the name of their town again? I can't remember."

Doc grinned. "Clover Hill."

Cade shot off a text to the number Doc had given him and then got on his bike. It was a nice, warm April evening and he enjoyed the feeling of the wind in his hair.

It only took a few minutes for him to get home—plenty of time for his excitement to ramp up.

By the time he walked in the door, his stomach was rumbling, though. His therapist had long since taught him not to make any big decisions on an empty stomach, especially after a full day of work. He needed to make dinner and he needed to talk to the one person who would be able to help take care of the living things in his apartment.

Cade pulled out his phone again and dialed a number he'd had memorized since he was ten. "Hey, Michael. Do you have dinner plans? I've got something I need to talk about and could use your advice."

His on-again-off-again ex-boyfriend and lifelong best friend agreed easily, though he made Cade promise to cook for him when he got there. Cade didn't mind that so much, since the meal subscription boxes had arrived yesterday.

While he waited for Michael, Cade changed out of his work clothes and into another set of joggers and a tank top that showed off his tattoos. Then, he set about tending to his plants and his aquarium.

Cade had started keeping plants after his parents divorced as a kid. He wasn't allowed to have a pet of his own to take between their apartments, so his dad had taken him to Home Depot and let him pick out the plants for a window box. He had fallen in love for the first time in his life. Ever since, he'd had at least a few air plants in every place he'd lived, slowly building his collection of beauties until his apartment looked... well, like an indoor jungle.

The actions of siphoning the water and fish poop from the bottom of the tank into the oversized watering can to reuse for the various plants in his apartment was soothing.

Turning each of the plants so all of their leaves were able to easily get the sun and nutrients they needed had always helped him to clear his mind, and tonight was no exception.

When Michael arrived, he didn't bother knocking. He just waltzed in and beelined for the freshwater aquarium in the living room. "Hello, my little fishies. I brought you some treats!" As if they knew what was coming, all the fish swam to the front of the tank while Michael revealed a few frozen cubes of bloodworms. "Who's your favorite parent? Yes, it's me."

Cade couldn't help but laugh as he leaned in the doorway to the kitchen. He was fairly certain the fish didn't think about parenthood so much, but he did like to see Michael caring for the fish he'd brought home so long ago.

When the fish had devoured the bloodworms, Michael turned to where Cade leaned and put his hands on his suit-clad hips. "Now, what's up with the non-favorite fish parent? You sounded weird when I called."

"Silly Michael. I'm always weird." Cade laughed. "Come on, I'll tell you while I make dinner."

Dinner was a chopped chili chicken stir fry. All he had to do was chop, mix and cook while he talked. With Michael that had always been easy, and tonight was no different.

"I mean, all of that sounds fun," he said when Cade finished. "I don't really see a big problem, other than you'd be away from me for *soooo* long."

The pout on Michael's lips as he dragged out the word 'so' made Cade laugh, as his friend had surely intended.

The rice cooker beeped, and Cade served up two bowls. Michael took his with a nod of thanks.

"I mean, I'm a little worried about what might happen if it turns out I'm only good here, with Doc? What if I can't do what they need me to do for Bryan's new place and the business fails?"

Michael's face turned serious as he thought through what Cade had said. "I understand your concern. But I have a question to counterbalance it. Well, a couple. What if it *doesn't* fail?"

Cade's hand froze halfway to his mouth, the stir fry falling off his fork. He didn't know what to say, so Michael kept talking.

"What if it turns out you're great at it and it turns into something with a little more opportunity for growth for you? I know you love what you do, but... what if you love this, too?"

The positive twist on all his worries stunned him. Michael was right. He could be good at this. It was exactly the foil he needed to clear the tiny, lingering anxiety away.

"So... is that you volunteering to take care of everything here while I'm gone?"

Michael's booming laugh filled the room. "Gladly, you weirdo."

two

. . .

"I quit!" Daphne flung her handful of papers onto the coffee table with the frustration of an overtired toddler. "Obviously, there are no good roommates left in the world. You were the last one. I'll just have to live alone for all eternity."

Her best friend didn't even look at her. Kavanaugh was preoccupied with petting the purring gray ball of fur curled in their lap. When they did look up at the scattered papers, they rolled their eyes.

Daphne knew she was being melodramatic, but really, she didn't think she was asking for too much from her prospective roommates. She needed someone who was okay with cats, financially stable enough to pay their share of the rent, and wouldn't make it difficult for her to run her wedding planning business.

This was what she got for advertising in the Firhaven classifieds and on Craigslist for Baymill, but what else could one do when even Mrs. Quintanilla didn't know anyone in need of a place to stay?

"I'm sure there's someone good in the pile of

applications. They don't have to be as cool as Kavanaugh. They just have to pay rent," Bryan said from where he sat cross-legged in the papasan chair.

"Thanks for the stunning glimpse of the obvious, bud." Daphne's sarcasm was biting as she paced the room, but Bryan knew better than to take her seriously. He stuck his tongue out at her and they both laughed.

She hadn't exactly been overly picky. There had been two potential options, but they'd both fallen apart at the walkthrough stage. The first had turned out to have a previously undiagnosed cat allergy that had flared up when she pet Sushi, and the second had given both her and Kav extremely bad vibes. They'd decided to trust their guts on that one and declined the application.

"What if you've spoiled me for all other roommates? I mean, it's been almost fifteen years since I've lived with anyone else." They had been friends since elementary school, and roommates since their sophomore year of college

A lot had changed since they'd first become friends. To start with, they weren't seven anymore. Both of them had had big dreams for their adult lives, but most had fallen apart with the realization that no, it wasn't realistic for them to own adjoining islands or run a training school for unicorns.

Unfortunately, magic wasn't real, so they were stuck with their mundane realities.

They had made the most of it, even when they were living in their very first shithole apartment up in Baymill during college. All the adventures had made them stronger friends, strong enough to know their friendship would survive Kavanaugh's latest adventure—moving out and getting ready to marry Bryan.

Thus the roommate search. She'd thought the emotional part would be harder than the logistical aspects, but both Kav and Bryan had made it clear in the weeks they'd been gone that Daphne would always be welcome in their new home. It cushioned the newfound loneliness. The distinct lack of potential roommates to split the rent and bills with was another matter entirely.

Kav sighed. "Why don't you let me take a look? Maybe I can help pull out the least terrible options so you can come back with fresh eyes later?"

Daphne shrugged. "Have at it. I'm getting a glass of wine. Bryan, Kav, you want some lemonade?"

They both nodded. Kav lifted themself off the couch with a stretch and a groan, a move echoed by the floppy-eared cat.

"Oh, what a biiiiig stretch," Kav complimented Sushi.

The cat rubbed up against them as if she appreciated being noticed. Now it was Daphne's turn to roll her eyes. Daphne may be spoiled for roommates, but the cat was just plain spoiled.

She headed into the kitchen to get the drinks, but startled at the sound of Bryan's phone playing "Piano Man."

He squeaked loudly. "My dad's office manager is calling! He might actually want to come help us get set up." He followed her into the kitchen, phone pressed to his ear as he asked the person on the other end of the line to hold while he got somewhere he could talk. Tapping the screen, he turned to Daphne, whispering, "Okay for Sushi to come out with me, Daph?"

Daphne shrugged. He was as good at keeping an eye on her as any of them were. She slid the door shut behind them. She made her way back out to the living room and set the drinks on the table next to the now-neat pile of papers.

She bent to sit cross-legged next to Kav, but nearly fell over when she heard a loud *thunk* coming from the patio door. Daphne looked up to see Bryan waving one of his arms wildly and pointing out at the backyard with the other.

"What in the hell?" Daphne sped over the door, only to gasp at the sight of a furry gray cat ass sprinting for the treeline.

Fuck.

Daphne's brain kicked into focus mode. She slid her feet into the flip flops she always kept by the door. "Kav, Sushi made a run for it again! I'll follow her, you get the carrier and meet me at Reuben's."

She could hear Kav scrambling after her, which was good because she had very little time to catch the creature before she hit Lovegrass Street. Until her parents had showed up with Sushi, she had thought kittens would be slow. After all, they had pretty stubby legs, and they had to be uncoordinated since they were so young.

Boy, had she been wrong there. This was now the fourth time Sushi had escaped. At least this time, they'd realized it before she'd been gone for long. The first time, she had been gone nearly four hours before they'd found her, tucked neatly under the dumpster at Reuben's, happily lapping at the remains of a bowl of ice cream.

Every time she'd gotten out since then, she'd headed right back in that direction. Tonight seemed to be no exception.

Daphne would be impressed if she wasn't so annoyed that this would mean yet another set of stained clothes. Why couldn't Sushi make a run for it on a night when she was in junky clothes?

The answer was because she didn't actually own anything that would have fit any definition of junky, let alone anything that wouldn't be harmed by crawling under a dumpster. Daphne tugged her silk blouse tighter to her body and tucked it into the waistband of her pencil skirt so she could move with the speed she needed without worrying about catching it on tree branches.

She knew she looked ridiculous, but all she could do now was follow the cat and pray none of the neighbors were looking out their back windows tonight.

Despite the cool breeze, Daphne was sweaty, disheveled, and out of breath by the time she reached Reuben's. Sushi hadn't stopped for even a sniff on her three-block sprint, so neither had Daphne. Sure enough, though, as soon as she had the chance, the brat found herself a snack and squirmed to the farthest corner of the space under the dumpster.

Daphne didn't bother trying to pull herself together. She squatted next to the dumpster and put her hands on her wide hips to try and make it easier to catch her breath. The sound of the cat lapping at something she definitely shouldn't be eating was *irksome*.

As if on cue, the headlights from Kav's SUV flashed over her. A moment later, she heard a door slam and footsteps come closer.

Kav squatted down next to her and set the cat carrier

between them. "If she's gonna keep raiding the empty ice cream containers, maybe you should talk to Reuben about making her the company mascot."

That made Daphne laugh. "I don't think he would go for that. You know how much of a curmudgeon he can be."

"Yeah, but who could resist such a cutie? She'd have to be good for business." They pitched their voice higher and cooed into the area under the dumpster. "Yes, you would, wouldn't you? Even if you are a tiny furry asshole. Yes you are."

The cat replied with an indignant *prrt*, then went back to her snack. Furry asshole, indeed.

Daphne glared under the dumpster. "Ma'am, you have perfectly good snacks at home. We even have ice cream at home. Why do you feel the need to eat it *here*?"

"Well, she's a cat. They like to be contrary. It's why you like them. And partially why you like me."

"Oh, only partially?" Daphne raised an eyebrow that Kavanaugh probably couldn't see in the waning light.

"Partially. The other reason is because I always come armed with snacks." They pulled out a bag of Sushi's favorite treats from one coat pocket and a bag of pretzels from the other. "We're all set to hang out for a while now, whatever it takes to get Sushi."

Daphne laughed until tears welled in her eyes. She should have known Kav would be prepared for anything. That was their way.

The realization that she would have to do things like this on her own more often than not, that she'd have to prepare herself for any possible scenario rather than relying on her best friend... that made the tears flow for real.

Kav folded their legs underneath them and sat next to Daphne, reaching across the cat carrier to take both her hands in theirs. The touch was warm and comforting, just like their voice. "Whoa, hey, there's no need to cry. Sushi will come out, the same as she always does. We'll get her home."

"But you've moved out! I can't simply call you whenever the cat gets out, or there's a spider, or I'm not sure what to make for dinner. You're living with him and have a whole life on your own."

Kav sucked in a breath. If Daphne could see more clearly, she might think she saw tears in her best friend's eyes. But Kav never cried.

"Our relationship is going to change a little now that I'm getting married, sure, but I'm not cutting you off. In fact, I insist you call me whenever the cat gets out or you don't know what to make for dinner. That part of our relationship doesn't have to change. You know that, right? Plus, we're only a few streets away, and we're building a business for the long haul here."

Daphne remained a little baffled they thought Clover Hill was large enough for a dedicated chiropractic clinic. It still seemed so small to her, the way it had been when she was growing up. But it had grown nicely over the years. Now they had a second tea shop downtown (one for boba, and one with cupcakes), a couple bars, and even more new businesses popping up every day.

Hell, even the local wedding planning business had picked up enough for her to go out on her own when she'd lost her job at Merino Events. She guessed she *did* understand how a chiropractor would fit in.

"You really have that much faith in this guy? I thought

you said he was a golden retriever in the form of a physical therapist."

"Well, he is, but he also runs Bryan's dad's practice extremely well. We've heard stories about him for years, and to hear Doc tell it, he's helped make some big changes and ensure every patient gets the care they need, no matter what they can pay. That's exactly what we want for this place."

"It sounds great," she said sincerely.

"It will be. And you know I'm here for you, no matter what. Bryan knows the rules and he doesn't want to come between us, ever. We're a package deal."

The words warmed Daphne's heart. Apparently, it warmed Sushi's, too. She chose that moment to crawl out from under the dumpster. The creature came to a halt right in front of her open carrier, licking her chops at her stolen spoils.

They rode home with the radio on, singing quietly. Sushi joined in, yowling at top volume, as usual. She hated to be in the car, but given what she'd just put them through, Daphne didn't care.

When they pulled up to the curb, a quick glance at the house-turned-duplex showed that their neighbor/landlord wasn't home. Judging by the Slenderman-like shadow in their bottom corner apartment, Bryan had gone back inside. And he was moving very oddly.

Daphne watched in shock as his shadow threw its arms and legs around in a pattern she couldn't identify. Was he being robbed? Was there a spider? Or—

"Holy shit, he's dancing," Kav breathed. "Here's hoping that's a good sign. Quick, let's get inside."

Kav turned the car off and Daphne hopped out with the cat carrier. They rushed down the white stone path to the front door and barged in.

Bryan whooped with sheer delight when he saw Sushi. "I'm so glad you got her back. Now the evening is officially perfect!"

"The call went well, then? He's going to come help?" Daphne let the still-yowling cat out of the carrier.

"Yes he is!" He swept his fiancé up into an exuberant kiss that filled the room with a feeling of love and warmth. When Bryan set Kav down, he turned toward Daphne. "And he's gonna need a place to stay. Obviously, no pressure, but I think we might have found the solution to your roommate problem."

Daphne blinked. Surely he couldn't mean what she thought he meant.

"I didn't make any promises, and I'm gonna put him in a hotel for at least the first couple days, but he's agreed to stay for three months and Pop is gonna pay his rent. If you like him... maybe we could solve two problems with one room, so to speak?"

That... didn't sound terrible. The more Daphne thought about it, the more she liked the idea. This guy fit all of her criteria and she knew Bryan's Pop was good for the rent. She also knew that if he gave off a bad vibe, Bryan would accept it and find him somewhere else to live.

As long as he passed the vibe check, she felt like she could deal with anyone Kav liked for three months. The least she could do was to meet this 'trans golden retriever gym bro' when the time came.

Which gave her an idea. "Why don't you bring him here for dinner the night he gets in? So he can see the place and meet Sushi and me and you'll all get a good meal in before you take him to… where, Bluestem?"

Bryan nodded, his brow knit in thought. "Are you sure you're comfortable with that? Having someone new in your space is hard and we can always host dinner at our house, or out somewhere if it's easier."

She smiled at him and watched his face smooth out. "I wouldn't offer if I didn't mean it, Bry. This way he'll get the full experience of the McGee household before either of us makes a decision."

Bryan wrapped her up in a hug. "Thank you, Daphne. I really appreciate it."

"As you should. I am excellent," she joked. "Now, bring me my wine and let's play a round of spoons. I'm ready to kick your asses again."

three

. . .

Two weeks later, Cade found himself standing in the Fairview Regional Airport looking for his new boss.

Luckily, there were maybe three gates and a single coffee shop with no line inside the terminal. It made it easy to spot the lanky man waiting for him with a wide smile on his face. Beside him was another familiar person with a similar smile on their face as they both waved enthusiastically.

"Dr. Schwartz, Kav, it's good to see you again."

"Please, call me Bryan," the man said.

Cade nodded and held out his hand to shake professionally, but Bryan took it and enveloped him in an unexpected, but not unwelcome, hug. It surprised a laugh out of him, but he hugged back.

"Bryan, give the man some space," Kav said after a moment, gently nudging him with an elbow. Bryan released Cade and laughed with them both, rubbing a hand along the back of his neck in clear embarrassment.

"Sorry, sorry. I'll ask next time I want to hug you, I

19

promise. I am so glad you decided to come help us out! And I get to show you our awesome town!"

His enthusiasm was contagious. Cade couldn't help but grin back at them both. "Well, let's get to it, then! I can't wait to see Clover Hill."

They led him out of the airport and to an older, yet pristine, green SUV, asking him several times if there was anything he needed. He declined. He'd used the restroom and he'd eaten on the plane. It would have been nice to grab a shower after several hours packed into a too-small plane seat like a sardine in a can, but he would survive without one.

Wind blew across the back of his neck and he was regretting the fade he'd gotten right before he'd left. Sure, it made him look more clean cut, but it was way colder here than it had been when he'd left Raleigh, despite the sun beating down on their heads.

Luckily, it didn't take long to get his single bag into the trunk. His companions insisted he take the passenger seat so he could have the best view while Kavanaugh drove and Bryan clambered into the middle of the backseat. His legs were so long he barely fit, but it didn't seem to faze him.

Kav rolled their eyes at their partner, then grinned at Cade almost wolfishly. "I hope you don't get carsick. We've got a little bit of a hike ahead of us, and I don't intend to waste any time by driving slowly. No matter how long it takes, Bry's gonna talk your ear off about his business plan the whole time."

Bryan leaned forward and pressed a kiss to their cheek. "They've got that right. I'm a talker! You're probably used to it from working with my Pop. We've got some different plans, though."

He started with a review of what they'd talked about on the phone—a combination of the traditional chiropractor and physical therapy clinic with a space for some basic exercise classes taught by the team. Cade chimed in with a few ideas of his own for the content of the classes, and was gratified when Bryan wrote them down in a notebook that seemed worse for wear.

They might have given him the passenger seat for the best view, but he spent most of it looking at his new boss. The more he talked, the more exuberant his gestures and smiles got. Kav occasionally chimed in with details Bryan hadn't remembered, but that was it until they pulled off the highway onto an unmarked gravel road, and then to an abrupt halt.

Cade glanced between them, wondering for a moment if maybe he should have listened to Michael's concerns about stranger danger and gotten his own rental car. "Did you bring me out here to kill me? If so, can you be convinced otherwise?"

Kavanaugh and Bryan laughed in unison, just as he'd intended. "Look out your window. I wanted to make sure your first look at Clover Hill was the best one, and this is it."

He turned away from them and sucked in a breath.

Rolling hills rose out of the surrounding farmland, and the highest was dotted with a variety of older brick buildings and newer chrome and concrete ones. The further out he looked from that central area, the more different the styles of buildings became. None seemed to go together, but somehow it created a patchwork quilt effect that took his breath away.

He didn't know how long he sat there taking it all in. Eventually, one of his companions cleared their throat.

Cade pulled his eyes away from the town to glance at them. Neither were trying to hide the joy on their faces, but Cade was worried by a glint in his new employer's eye.

The worry turned to self-consciousness as he ran a hand over his hair. Had he stared for too long? Was his reaction not what they'd expected? Did they think he was weird?

After a few too many seconds of silence, he blurted out, "What is that look for?"

Kav answered instead of their partner. "I can't wait to see your face when you see it up close. I have a feeling you're going to fit into Clover Hill just fine."

Somehow, he was starting to get that feeling, too.

After a quick tour of Clover Hill and dropping his bags off at the Bluestem Bed and Breakfast, Cade had to admit he was impressed. The town was larger than he had expected, but at every stoplight and passenger crossing in their path, at least one person had waved or called a hello. It gave it a small-town feel that showed the truth of every kind thing he'd been told about it.

Finally, though, they pulled into the driveway of a gingerbread-style Victorian house.

"This is where dinner and Daphne are," Bryan smiled over his shoulder. "And your new home, if all goes well."

No pressure or anything, Cade thought wryly. He looked past them to study the home. It had clearly once been a grand and glamorous estate, with so many rows of hedges separating its yard from the other houses on the street, but judging by the two differently colored front doors and the polar-opposite styles of curtains on the windows on either side of the house, at some point it had clearly been split into two apartments.

The landscaping, however, was all-inclusive. Several different kinds of bushes with purple, blue, and pink flowers guided the three of them onto the wraparound porch, where wisteria climbed the wrought iron railing and onto the roof. Everywhere there weren't planters, clover spread all over the yard. It looked like it could've been pulled straight from a book of fairy tales.

He wondered, for the first time, if maybe he wouldn't fit in in this house. He didn't know how he and his weights would fit into anything as beautiful as this, let alone with a woman who kept it up. He had a lot of plants at home, but he let them grow as long as they were healthy. This was manicured, aside from the wisteria. No one could keep that vine down.

Kavanaugh and Bryan clearly had no such qualms, though. They led him to the royal blue front door and knocked three times before letting themselves in. "Daphne, we're here!"

Cade followed them in, slid his shoes off next to the rack, and stared.

The living room looked like it had been pulled straight out of a magazine, and had way more space than he'd anticipated from the exterior of the house.

The entryway was walled on either side, but from what he could tell, those were the only interior walls in the downstairs part of the apartment. He could see straight across the living room, with its cherry wood furniture decorated with pops of dusty pinks, blues, and mustard, to the staircase which had to lead to the bedrooms.

Through a framed opening to his left, he could see the

kitchen—and a voluptuous blonde woman in a tailored maroon pantsuit standing precariously on the top step of a ladder that leaned on the dining room table. She was cursing a blue streak under her breath, getting louder every time the ladder beneath her wobbled.

He wanted to help, but hesitated. He knew if he ran over there as a large male stranger, he was more likely to freak her out than be of any help. She, however, had no such qualms.

"You! Giant man! Help me hold this in place!"

He snapped into movement at the command in her voice, running over and reaching to grab the colored glass light fixture from her so she could focus on her balance.

"No! What are you doing? Hold the ladder, not the light. I've got this part."

Praying she couldn't see the way his face burned, he let go of the light and moved to stand behind the ladder. He gripped it with both hands, hoping that would help it stay standing.

He watched her struggle for almost thirty seconds before he decided it was worth saying something. "Um, if you move the ladder a little closer, you'll probably have a better chance of reaching. Would you like my help?

"No. I've got it. I just need to get... a little... taller..." She stretched herself out between each word and wobbled, trying to hook the fixture into its base. The next thing he knew, she was falling hard and fast. Without taking even a heartbeat to think, he lowered his knees and reached out his arms, hoping to God he could catch her without breaking either of them.

four

. . .

The world shifted into slow motion as Daphne crashed toward the floor. She cringed in anticipation of the pain that would come from hitting the hard wood, but she never touched it. Instead, the man she'd asked to hold the ladder was... holding her. His arms were wrapped around her like the bar on a roller coaster ride. His body hit the ground, but all she felt was the breath whooshing out of him a split second before hers did the same.

They lay on the ground for what felt like an eon. Daphne was trying to remember how to breathe, and she was sure the giant man she was lying on was doing the same.

She opened her eyes with a jolt. She was lying on top of him. She could feel the press of his stomach, and the lines of muscles in his arms and legs against hers. And she couldn't stay there.

She tried to get up, but had to drop back down. His arms were too tight around her to let her go far. Cade let out a *whoof* as the weight of her knocked the wind back out of him.

She turned her head so she could look at him. "Sorry, I'm so sorry. It's just… you're still holding onto me."

He flushed from the tops of his ears down to the vee of his collar and released her.

The next time she tried to roll off him, there was no resistance. She brushed herself off vigorously, as if to rid herself of the feel of his arms and dust all at the same time. Really, though, her waist felt colder somehow than it had before, as if it missed the touch.

There was no time to focus on it, though. Kav and Bryan rushed in then. Bryan grabbed the ladder from the floor next to them and Kav helped Daphne to her feet.

"What the hell happened? Are you two okay?"

Daphne took a quick inventory of her body. Aside from being a little winded, there wasn't anything wrong with her. "I'm fine, I think. I landed pretty hard on your new physical therapist, though. Are you okay?"

The man blinked at her from the floor.

"Cade? Are you okay?" Bryan's voice was worried as he leaned over. "Do we need to call an ambulance?"

"No, no, I'm fine," he groaned in a way that clearly said he was not. "I might need a hand up, though."

Daphne and Bryan instantly held theirs out, and he took one of each. As he pulled himself up, she was glad Bryan was helping because he felt even heavier than he looked.

But then she realized, of course he would. She was unequivocally fat herself, but he was nearly a foot taller than her, and a little wider with way more muscle.

Bryan cleared his throat, and she jumped. How long had she been staring at his chest?

"Are you okay? I didn't crush anything important, did I?" She didn't know which parts she'd fallen on, but she knew the weight of a human body falling on another had to hurt.

He simply smiled down at her, a deep dimple on one cheek visible just above the line of his soft-looking beard, and the worry turned into butterflies. Shit, he was handsome, too.

"I'll be fine. I'm just sore. I don't think the light fixture and your table can say the same, though."

She turned to look at the mess that now covered her table and winced. He was right. The antique milk glass was shattered across the center of the table and the floor, with the addition of crumbles of drywall, insulation and stray wires.

Mrs. Spencer was not gonna be happy about this, she thought sadly. The older woman who owned the house was very attached to it. But that was a later problem. After all, she wasn't even in the country right now.

"Well, I guess we're eating outside. Good thing it's a nice night. Kav, can you give Cade the grand tour while I clean this up? I don't want Sushi getting into this and eating something."

Kav opened their mouth to—hopefully—agree, but Cade's deeper voice came out first. "That's not necessary. I helped make the mess, so you shouldn't have to clean it up alone. Show me where your broom and dustpan are." Daphne propped her hands on her hips, intending to remind him he was a guest and she was the one who'd made it. But he held up one large, thick-fingered hand to stop her. "Really, I insist."

She wasn't going to argue with a man who insisted on cleaning. Kav directed him to the pantry, then got out of his way. Each movement he made seemed entirely fluid and purposeful, even the way his round ass swayed.

He turned around with the broom in hand and she blinked, realizing that she'd been staring. And her cheeks were hot. How embarrassing. She turned to hide her blush and to grab the trash can.

She didn't know what had come over her. She'd always appreciated beauty, but it usually took longer for her to notice anyone's backside. Then again, she also tried to avoid literally falling into people's arms before she'd introduced herself.

Oh god, she still hadn't introduced herself. She couldn't let that go on. "I'm Daphne, by the way. Thanks for catching me."

He looked up from his sweeping and smiled at her again. The reappearance of that dimple took her breath away almost as quickly as the fall had.

"I guessed. Nice to meet you, Daphne. I'm Cade, your potential roommate. Sorry about the mess."

She waved a handful of drywall at him. "This was not your fault. It was all me. I'm the one who got on a ladder that clearly wasn't sturdy enough to hold me and didn't get down when it wobbled."

"Well, then I'm glad it wasn't worse."

"It could have been if Cade hadn't kicked the ladder away when you came down," Bryan chimed in. Daphne whirled to find him studying the pieces of the ladder he'd cleared away. It looked much sharper than she'd ever expected it to. And twisted, somehow.

"Holy shit." Daphne and Cade spoke at the same time, then flashed looks at each other.

"Well, it looks like I owe you even more thanks than I thought," Daphne breathed, then snapped out her hand. "Hand me that broom. I changed my mind. You're not allowed to do housework tonight."

"What?" Cade was baffled. He could see by the steely look on her face that she was serious.

"You heard me. You saved the day, so no more house-work. Kav and Bryan can give you the grand tour, like I wanted to start with."

He opened his mouth to argue, then took another look at her face and handed over the broom with a grunt of surrender.

"Look at his face!" Bryan laughed. "You've hurt his feelings, Daph!"

Daphne stuck her tongue out at him, making them all laugh.

Bryan stepped forward and clapped a hand on Cade's shoulder. "Come on, man. You can help me take this night-mare of a ladder outside, and then I'll give you the tour."

Cade looked at him, then back at the fierce, beautiful woman wielding the broom like a weapon of war, then back at his new boss. Bryan shrugged at him.

So he grabbed the other piece of the ladder and followed Bryan out the back door.

"Garbage day isn't until Tuesday, so we can't leave this at the curb yet. Follow me."

Bryan led him down porch steps that matched the front and around the house to a hedged-in area clearly designed to hide things they didn't want to be seen from the road. The viburnum hedge was blooming with small, white flowers that looked at odds with the thorns he knew would be deeper inside the bush.

Bryan guided him around the corner, both making sure to set the pieces where no one would accidentally injure themselves, and then stepped back.

"Do you actually want a tour? There's not much to see out back."

Cade looked around, seeing the almost labyrinthine landscaping.

"Nah, I'm good. I gotta ask, though, does Daphne do all of the upkeep on the exterior? This seems like a lot."

Bryan snorted a laugh as he guided him back up to the porch.

"Not a chance. Tabitha Spencer, the landlord, hires a landscaper to take care of all of this. Daphne is great with people and animals, but has never even been able to keep cactuses and succulents alive for more than a few days. It's almost impressive.

She couldn't keep a plant alive? *Any* plant? That seemed impossible to him. Plants were so simple. All they needed was the right amount of water, sun and air. He'd always had a knack for them. People and animals... they were way more complicated.

"Don't get me wrong, though. She's amazing at a lot of other things. I mean, the interior decorating is all hers, and the events she plans are magical. I've never met anyone like her."

That was certainly something Cade couldn't have done. He could follow instructions well enough, and he knew he could pick decent colors to make a place look nice, but that was about it. He'd have to take a closer look at the house as he walked through. Cade may have lost his chance at making a good first impression, but at least he could make a good second one by giving her a compliment on something she obviously enjoyed.

"By the way, do you know if she has a partner?" He asked.

Bryan looked at him sharply, so he rushed to cover his

question. "J—Just so I can prepare myself if I decide to move in?"

There. That was something a normal roommate might ask. Not just someone who thought his possible new roommate was extremely attractive.

"I see. Well, I don't usually talk to my employees about my friends' dating lives, but she is single. As, I believe, are you?"

Cade nodded.

"Well. Good to know, I guess."

Cade smiled, turning back to the door in front of him. When he opened it, though, he felt something slide against his pant leg.

"What the—"

"Sushi, come back here!" he heard Kavanaugh shout from inside the house. He turned around and spotted a small gray form sprinting toward the tree line at the back of the property. That must be the cat Bryan had mentioned. He couldn't be responsible for breaking her ladder *and* letting her cat escape in the same hour.

Without another thought, he ran after the fuzzy creature. It ran faster than he had expected, and in a pattern that would have been difficult to follow even for someone who knew the landscape. Thanks to turning down the real tour, he didn't. Right as he got close enough that he thought he might be able to herd the cat back toward the house, he tripped over some paving stones and fell face-first into a mulched section

"At least it wasn't the viburnum," he muttered as he pulled himself into a sitting position.

Somehow, despite the sound he must have made, when he looked up he found himself staring into the cat's green eyes. Slowly, steadily, he reached forward and grabbed the cat.

It yowled and tried to escape him with claws that felt extremely sharp for such a small creature, but he kept it tucked against his chest as he got up and made his way back to the house. "If you just calm down, this will be much easier, you know," he said in a tone he hoped was soothing. It didn't seem to have any effect on the cat. *Oh, well.*

Bryan, Kav and Daphne were standing on the porch gaping at him.

"How did you catch Sushi so fast?" Daphne demanded when he'd transferred the cat to her arms. "Usually by the time I can get her, she's well on her way to Reuben's!"

That was the ice cream shop, if he remembered right from the tour. *At least she had good taste in her escape plans.*

That's when he really looked at the cat for the first time. Sushi's ears were... folded over on themselves.

He blurted the words out before he could stop them "Why are her ears like that? Did I hurt her?"

Daphne looked down at the cat in alarm, then her blonde brows lowered when she looked back up at him. "You mean the folds?"

Cade nodded. When Daphne started laughing, his own brows drew down.

"Oh, no! I'm sorry, I shouldn't laugh. She's a Scottish Fold. Their ears just do that. You've never seen one before?"

He shook his head, now thoroughly embarrassed. He'd never even heard of a Scottish Fold, and now he looked like he didn't know anything.

Well, at least he'd caught the cat. The evening wasn't a total loss.

"How about we set the table for dinner while you get her settled?" Kavanaugh asked.

Daphne nodded. "Sounds great. All the fixings are in the fridge."

Cade felt like this was a good time to make himself useful, to make up for how he'd felt ridiculous all evening. "Do you need me to help carry anything?"

"No," Daphne and Kavanaugh said at once.

Kavanaugh was the one to continue, though. "You've done more than enough for someone who's supposed to be the guest of honor. Let us get you dinner."

He couldn't argue there, so he sat down at one of the seats at the outdoor table. She smiled at him, and it had all the brightness of a happy lamp before she turned back to the house.

"And you, young lady, are going to my room. 'Cause I don't trust you."

He laughed as she walked away. A few seconds later, he spied her through the wide kitchen window. The light from the setting sun outlined her shoulder-length blonde waves and curvy silhouette in deep orange.

The sight took his breath away as much as their fall had earlier, and he wasn't sure exactly why. He'd known she was beautiful from the first glimpse, but he barely knew this woman. This dinner, which had been a source of anxiety before, now felt more like an opportunity.

Kav and Bryan had brought out most of the dinner's fixings and silverware by the time Daphne got back downstairs.

All that was left to carry out was the crockpot full of

chili that had been cooking all day. It smelled delicious, if she did say so herself.

Cade, apparently, agreed. His stomach rumbled the instant she set the pot on the table and he blushed a beautiful peach color with clear embarrassment. It was an adorable expression on such an attractive, muscular man.

"It's been a long time since my snack on the airplane."

"Well, then let's not keep you waiting."

Bryan and Kav sat on either side of him at the square table, leaving the chair directly opposite him for Daphne. She sat and Bryan immediately began doling out the chili into her favorite ceramic bowls and handing them around. Without any muss or fuss, they each crafted their bowls the way they wanted from the variety of fixings she'd prepared earlier that morning.

She chose sour cream, crispy fried onions and a ton of cheese for hers, and dug in.

Damn, for the five recipes I can consistently manage, I'm pretty good, she thought proudly.

Judging by the pleased *hmms* and lack of conversation around the table, the others thought so, too. But the silence started to verge on awkward, and with so much having gone wrong over the course of the last hour, Daphne was not going to let dinner get weird if she could help it.

"So, Cade, what do you think of Clover Hill so far?"

He swallowed and took a drink before he answered. Miss Manners would've been proud. "From what I saw on the tour today, it's a great town. I was anticipating a little more of a hokey small town from Doc's description."

The words made them all laugh. Daphne could imagine Bryan's Pop's thoughts on their town compared to the metropolitan area he lived in.

"I wouldn't say the town isn't totally hokey," Bryan

laughed. "After all, half the businesses in town have punny names."

"He says, as if his own business isn't going to have a pun in its name," Kav teased.

Cade looked at his boss in clear surprise, fork halfway to his mouth. It was apparent Bryan had not shared the name he had chosen. Daphne and Kav stared pointedly at him with matching raised eyebrows until he set his fork down indignantly.

"Cracked Up Chiropractic is the perfect name, thank you very much. It's fun and it'll be easy to market!" Bryan's voice was indignant and serious.

Cade snorted a laugh that turned into giggles so infectious Daphne couldn't help but join in.

"I think the patients will like it, too," he said when he'd stopped laughing. "I know most of mine would be cracking jokes about it, pun intended."

"See! The expert agrees, so quit bugging me about it!" Bryan crowed proudly.

Kav rolled their eyes at their fiancé, as if they'd had the same discussion several times and come to the same conclusion. Cade shook his head at his new boss.

Daphne loved her friends, and somehow it felt right to have Cade here with them. "Now that you know the name of your business, be sure to let me know if there's anything in particular you want to see or do in town. I've lived here my whole life and know basically everything there is to know about this place. I've got a cake tasting on Sunday, but otherwise I'm flexible."

Cade smiled at her, showing his single dimple again. "I might have to take you up on that, especially if you'll agree to let me take your spare bedroom while I'm here."

It was bold of him to come right out and ask. Daphne had to admire him for it, among the other obvious reasons.

She also didn't have to think too hard about it. Even though very little had gone to plan that evening, one thing had been clear—Cade was a really good guy.

She could see herself living with him in a platonic way, and the rent would be paid. If nothing else changed from then on, she might make a new friend. If it did… well, she couldn't wait to see just what their future together would hold.

"Sure, you've proven yourself to be a worthy house-mate. When would you like to move in?"

"My stuff is supposed to arrive on Monday morning. How's that sound?"

She grinned at him. "Sounds perfect. I'll be here to help."

The rest of dinner was kind of a blur for Cade. They talked about the business a little bit and how Daphne's wedding planning business, Mint to Be, was going.

From what he gathered, it was going to be a busy summer with two large weddings. The first was for one of their childhood friends, and Daphne was very excited about it.

"Rook and Lily will be here all weekend visiting Rook's family so we're going to nail down a lot of the last details. Like the cake flavors and decorations."

"When is it again? I want to make sure we've both got it in our calendars."

He dug into his chili while all three of them pulled out

their phones and double-checked the date. It was three weeks away.

"That reminds me, I still need a pet sitter for the three days I'll be gone, since you two will be with me for most of it. I don't want to leave Sushi alone for that long."

"I could help with that," Cade blurted out.

Daphne looked up at him, seemingly startled by the offer.

"I mean, it just makes sense since I'll be living here. All you would need to do is show me what you need done. Unless you don't want me to?"

"Oh, you're right! That would be way easier than hiring someone else. There's no need to teach you tonight, though. Sushi's pretty easy and it'll only take a minute. Actually, hand me your phone."

Without thinking, he pulled it out of his back pocket, unlocked it and handed it to her.

She tapped her screen a few times before handing it to him with the new contact screen open. "We're gonna need each others' numbers if we're going to be living together."

He added his information, then paused to make sure it was correct. In a flash of genius, he added "Giant Man" to his name, then gave it back.

She took one look at it and snorted—exactly the reaction he'd been aiming for. She tapped a few buttons and his own phone buzzed in his pants pocket.

"There, now you have mine."

five

. . .

Daphne was weirdly nervous as she walked through the brightly colored glass doors of Tea & Cupcakes.

It was a familiar space, one she had been coming to since she was a child, and the scent of the brewed teas and the sugar of all the baked goods mixed together to make what Daphne imagined ambrosia would smell like.

She had been coming in even more often since she had left Merino Events. The huge regional event planning company had been a great place to work, until she made the fatal mistake of breaking up with the boss's daughter and realizing just how much more important the 'family' part was to the family business.

Since then, any time she had needed to meet with the handful of clients she had managed to salvage, she had done so in one of the private rooms of the pharmacy-turned-bakery.

It was eclectic but charming, kind of like the rest of the town, with its antique wooden pharmacist's shelves that now held different blends of tea in mismatched glass jars instead of medicines. A whitewashed brick wall decorated with children's art in gold frames separated the main dining area from the meeting rooms.

She had wanted to find her own space by now, but life and money had gotten in the way. Hopefully, between the two large weddings she had this summer and finally finding a new roommate, she would someday be able to pay for some of the things she had been putting off and take the time to find an office.

But she couldn't focus on that now. She had to prepare herself for her meeting with Rook and Lily.

Even though she had known Rook since they were little, she still had to treat xem like any other client. She barely knew Lily other than through social media and emails. Hopefully, she could fix that today while they tasted a ton of the cupcakes this bakery was famous for.

And as usual, they showed up fifteen minutes earlier than they had scheduled.

Rook would have looked like a fae creature if xie didn't bounce on xir toes with excitement every time xey took a step. Lily, round and short like a hobbit with waist-length forest green wavy hair that contrasted her golden skin beautifully, barely came up to her partner's shoulder, but seemed to float instead of touching the ground. They made an odd, but beautiful, couple.

Rook swept Daphne into a hug that lifted her off her toes and cracked her aching back all at once. It was the best hug she'd had in weeks.

"Daphne, it's been *forever!* It's so nice to see you in person. Doing all this via email is not the same."

"Yes, well, you're the one who chose to live in South Evelyn instead of Clover Hill and have your wedding smack in the middle of the two," she reminded xem.

The couple exchanged a loaded look that terrified

Daphne. That look said *changes*, and there was no time for changes now. "Don't tell me you're changing the location this close to the wedding. I mean, I'm sure I can find something, but it'll be way expensive on such short notice. You'll still be on the hook for all of the previous venue's deposits, and—"

Lily held up their hands. "Whoa. Breathe, Daphne. Nothing in the wedding is changing. We've decided we're moving to Clover Hill afterwards."

Daphne looked at them, blinked, then looked at Rook. "Wait, really? You're coming back?" Her voice came out as more of a squeal than she'd intended but she didn't care.

When Rook nodded, it was Daphne's turn to wrap xem in a bone-crushing hug and spin xem around. "Oh that's so exciting! What changed? I—"

Merrill stepped out of the room they had booked with raised brows and pointed to their watch, and Daphne closed her mouth. *Right. They were here for a cake tasting. Not just catching up.*

"But we are gonna talk about that later! Right now, the miraculous Merrill is going to help you choose the perfect cake for your perfect day. Step right this way."

When they reached the room the brightly dressed, pixie-like baker stood in front of, they found a round table, four chairs, and a wooden buffet table with six glass cloches on it. Five held pairs of beautifully decorated miniature cakes, and the last held two baked cheesecakes. That was all it needed to feel cozy and magical in a way only a bakery could.

She inspected the flavors while Merrill introduced themself to Lily and talked them through how the process would work. Each cloche was labeled with a sticker in

Merrill's spidery handwriting. They had really outdone themself.

The first cupcakes were typical wedding cake choices—plain vanilla cake with buttercream and red velvet with cream cheese frosting. She couldn't imagine this particular couple choosing either flavor, but it made sense to offer them. The other cakes were a more likely choice for Rook and Lily. One was an almond cake with coffee ganache and dark chocolate curls. Daphne was intrigued by a lemon thyme ginger cake with lemon and berry curds between each layer, topped with mascarpone frosting. Merrill had also made an apple spice cake with cinnamon buttercream and caramel drips. The final option was New-York-style baked cheesecakes with apple roses and caramel on the top. All of them looked delicious, and judging by the looks on Rook's and Lily's faces as they tried each, they tasted even better.

The couple went back and forth for several minutes, talking about the pros and cons of each flavor while Merrill and Daphne stayed quiet. This was their decision to make.

Eventually, they narrowed it down to two choices—the cheesecake and the lemon thyme ginger cake. From an event-planning perspective, the cake was the easier option. But Rook and Lily never did anything the easy way, so Daphne had no idea which they'd choose.

"Thank you so much for this, Merrill. We loved all of these," Lily said earnestly. "Would it be possible to have two sets of cakes? The miniature cheesecakes for the rehearsal dinner and the lemon thyme ginger cake for the actual wedding cake. Is that… is that possible?"

Merrill went entirely still in the seat beside Daphne.

She could almost see the panic blooming behind their neon purple octagonal frames.

"H-how many guests are you expecting for the rehearsal?" Merrill asked, clearing their throat. "Not that I'm against the idea, you understand, but we're a fairly small business and you mentioned you were expecting two hundred guests for the wedding."

Lily hurried to assure them that the rehearsal dinner definitely wasn't the full guest list. Rook turned to Daphne. "Was fifty the final number we settled on?"

Daphne flipped open the binder that was always at hand to double-check. "Yep! Fifty on the nose."

Merrill started to sag with what Daphne guessed was relief, but caught themself and smiled. "Then we can absolutely do that! It will add to the cost I originally quoted you, of course."

"Oh, we know. We'll work with Daphne to figure out where to pull the money from, but your prices are so reasonable that we're sure it will work perfectly." The couple beamed at Daphne, who felt a little queasy at the sudden change.

"All right, so miniature cheesecakes for the rehearsal dinner and then... you still wanted to go with the four tiers I recommended for your actual wedding cake, right? Or did you want to go bigger, since you were right on the cusp of the number of people it will feed?

When they agreed to four tiers, Merrill made a note and smiled more sincerely. "I will send you and Daphne an email shortly with the contract and all the prices."

Daphne grinned at them. "Then we'll get that back to you as soon as possible. Do you mind if we hang out in the room for a little while? We have a couple other items to discuss before I let these two loose on the town."

"All yours. Just let Ashton know when you're done and I'll come tidy up."

Daphne opened the budget pages and turned back to the couple. "Okay, before we get started with the budget, you two tell me everything about the upcoming move. I need all the details immediately."

Cade was already exhausted by the time he pulled his rental car up in front of his new home that morning.

The truck delivery driver with his small storage container of belongings was only a few seconds behind him. It had taken some arguing at the lot that morning, pointing out his car would not be able to tow anything, and a promise of twenty dollars to get the man to come with him.

But they'd both made it, and it was time to get his stuff moved in. Except he didn't have a key, and he didn't see Daphne's VW anywhere. He pulled his phone out of his too-tight back pocket and was getting ready to hit the call button when he heard the house's door creak open.

When he looked up, he saw Daphne standing there in a jumpsuit, with a smile on her face that made him think she'd been watching him for longer than he realized.

"I was about to call," he explained. "You don't have to help me move boxes. I just realized I never got a key."

"Cade Dawson, you may not have lived in a small town for long, but one thing you should know is we don't let our roommates move in unassisted. Now, tell me where to start."

When he rolled up the door of the storage unit a few seconds later, Daphne seemed surprised at how little was inside. Six medium moving boxes and a mattress were strapped in place with bungee cords to the back half of the unit. The front held only his bicycle.

He and Bryan had discussed furnishing options, and since Cade would be taking over his fiancé's old room, Kavanaugh had left most of their bedroom furniture for him rather than selling everything. The Bluestem had been their backup plan if he and Daphne hadn't gotten along, which also wouldn't have required furniture.

So all he had to bring for himself were the things he would need for a three-month stay—a variety of outfits for whatever being a consultant threw at him, a small selection of his weightlifting gear, the bedding he was attached to, his laptop, and a few personal decorations to make his space feel more like his own. Plus, of course, a mattress. He didn't have an issue with used furniture in general, but the idea of sleeping on his boss's partner's old mattress for three months gave him the heebie jeebies.

He unhooked the wheel locks from the bike and rolled it out, where Daphne took charge of it. While she walked it to the house, he unstrapped the rest of his belongings and moved them to the front of the unit.

From there, it was easy. He and Daphne grabbed two lighter boxes each and they made their way upstairs with only a few words of guidance on Daphne's part so he didn't run into the door frames or the railings.

He set his boxes down inside the walk-in closet, and turned to see Daphne squatting to set her own boxes down a few feet away.

She had great form. Combined with the way her clothes turned skintight with the movement… it made his mouth go dry. He wasn't sure he had ever seen something so beautiful.

She set the boxes down and he tore his eyes away. He couldn't let her know he found her extremely attractive on the day he moved in. That was weird and creepy.

Instead, he forced himself to look around the room that was now his home. It was larger than he'd expected for such an old house, with white and light gray painted stripes on the wall. Kav had made good use of the space with an eclectic collection of IKEA and what he guessed was thrifted or antique wooden furniture. All the wooden furniture was dark but warm, similar to the downstairs furniture. The IKEA furniture had been painted in a rainbow of colors around the room, making it feel bright and cheerful.

Daphne stood and must have noticed his perusal of the furniture. "If these aren't to your taste, we can always paint again."

The words were neutral but the slight frown on her plush lips told him she thought he didn't like the room.

"Oh, no! It's so bright and cheerful! You two have such a great eye for color. I mean, it looks kind of like an abstract progress flag. What could be cooler than that?"

He breathed a sigh of relief when his words brought the smile he already adored back to her face. "That's exactly what Kav wanted. They've got plans to get custom rainbow furniture once they're married to make sure the bedroom set all goes together. But this always makes me happy."

"I know the feeling well. That's why I got these tattoos over my top surgery scars." He waved at his chest and she raised an eyebrow. Looking down, he realized he was wearing a shirt and blushed. She couldn't see the tattoo he meant. But he could fix that. Without another thought, Cade lifted his shirt over his head so she could, then gestured at the tattooed vines that crossed just under where his breasts had once been. "See? They've got the trans flag colors in them!"

She blinked several times at his chest, never looking up at his face. He looked down at it again, wondering if there was something offensive on it. A bug maybe? But no, it was just his chest.

He liked the look of his chest. From the way his pectorals were slightly round before becoming part of his rounded belly, to the light dusting of blond hair over the expanse, he looked like a teddy bear. Judging by the look on her face, she wasn't having the same reaction.

Or... was she? She had leaned forward slightly to balance on her toes, and it looked like her face was flushed as her eyes traced the lines of his body. Was that... could it be... attraction?

His body began to warm at the thought of her fingers following the same path. He shook himself slightly, hoping to halt that line of thought in its tracks. That was a later thought, not a right-now thought. The movement seemed to bring Daphne back to herself, too.

"Your artist did beautiful work," she complimented him in a slightly husky voice. She cleared her throat, then stepped back. The distance between them didn't feel any less charged, though.

Cade blushed at the compliment and pulled his shirt back over his head. "Thank you. Later, I'll show you some of his other work. For now, we should probably, uh, finish moving the stuff in."

She nodded and walked out of the room at a measured pace. He sucked in a deep breath, trying to will his face back to its normal color before he followed after her.

Cade wasn't sure if it worked, but he knew his next box

would be heavy. He could always blame it on exertion if she called him on it. With that in mind, he made his way down the stairs and out the door, just in time to see her go for the box labeled 'equipment.'

The world seemed to slide into slow motion again as she tried to lift the box, and he tried to get her attention before she hurt herself lifting all of his weight set in one box. He pulled up short when he got to the unit and realized that she was lifting the box, and lifting it correctly. He could see her legs, glutes and arms flex from behind until she turned around.

"What, you think I can't lift weights like you can?" Her voice was a little out of breath, but clearly teasing, as though she knew she was not nearly as strong as he was. After that, he wasn't so sure.

"I meant for you to grab this other box with the bedding, but if you've got it…"

She didn't even let him finish the sentence. "Oh, hell no. You're the weight lifter. Lift your own weights."

He laughed and outstretched his arms to take the box. She slid it into his arms, making him grunt. It was a really heavy box. He really should have packed less efficiently and more realistically. The stairs were going to be hell.

And hell they were. He knew the dimensions of the staircase now, at least, so he bumped into less, but he was winded by the time he was able to set the box down in the closet.

Daphne, on the other hand, breezed in behind him like she didn't have a care in the world and set her box on top of his with a smug smile. She waited for him to catch his breath, then they both went back for the final item—the mattress.

Cade thanked the driver for waiting with a tip, and let

him know he could leave as soon as they'd unloaded the mattress. As a man of apparently few words, he just nodded.

Moving the mattress up the stairs was much easier by comparison, even with the awkwardness that came with moving any large object. Together, they pivoted and twisted until they got it through the door and let it fall onto the bed frame with a thump.

They both breathed a sigh of relief when it was in place. Cade wasted no time flopping onto it, enjoying not having to move for just a few seconds. He looked up to see Daphne walking out of the room.

"You don't have to leave, you know." He didn't want her to. She was the best moving buddy he'd ever had, and more beautiful by far.

"Oh, I know." She tossed her hair over her shoulder with the words, showing off her smile again. It took Cade's breath away as surely as the stairs had. "I just want to let Sushi out of my room, which means I have to close the front door."

Oh. That made sense, he supposed. He listened to her footsteps lightly tap down the stairs and the front door creak shut. A few seconds later, her footsteps came back up the stairs and passed his room to open what he guessed was her own bedroom door.

Seconds later, there was the feeling of a small, concentrated weight on the mattress. Turning his head, he was not surprised to see Sushi coming toward him, picking her way across the quilted top.

A snort from the doorway alerted him to Daphne's return. "Little traitor."

Cade smiled. "I'm sure I smell great to her, with how much I'm sweating. Plus I'm new. Care to join us?"

Daphne did, though she sat down with much more care than he had. Sushi abandoned him and made her way to her mother with a purr that seemed to come from a much larger cat.

"See, she knows who loves her."

She laughed. "You know, usually when I'm hot and sweaty on a mattress with a hot guy, I've had a lot more fun. And Sushi's not there."

The breath Cade had been taking turned into a cough, and then a laugh. Daphne laughed with him, though she hid her face behind the cat.

I guess that answers the question of whether it was attraction I saw earlier. "I'll try and make next time more fun for you. And less furry."

Daphne's brain had screeched to a halt at his teasing reply, though her body kept laughing somehow. Next time? Did he mean…. Was he attracted to her, too?

She was glad Sushi's body covered most of her face from view, because she was sure she had turned beet red. It was very possible that living with someone she found so attractive might actually kill her before their three months together were over.

"Do you want to go to dinner tonight?" The words were out of her mouth before she could stop them, and despite her desperate desire to do so, she couldn't take them back. She could only explain herself. "I mean. Once you're done unpacking. You just moved in and I have not gone grocery shopping, so there's basically nothing to eat in the house, so we should get dinner when you're done unpacking. As a celebration! Not as a date. Unless you want it to be a date?"

He was staring at her. She could feel the heat of his gaze on the side of her face.

"You don't have to make a decision right now. I'll leave you to start unpacking. My room is just at the end of the hall, so holler if you need anything or… if you make a decision. Just let me know!"

Turning on her heel, she walked out of the room and down the hall to her own, cursing herself. She couldn't believe she had said *any* of that. The man had *literally* just moved in and already she'd asked him out.

She pulled out her phone and clicked a contact before she could stop herself.

"Hello?" Kav's voice was gravelly, like they'd just woken up.

"Kav, it's me. I think I just did something incredibly unwise and I need you to help me fix it."

"What the hell time is it?"

Daphne looked at her alarm clock and saw it was only ten in the morning. She blinked. It had only been a few weeks, but she had forgotten how late Kav liked to sleep in.

This had been way easier when she could just barrel into her best friend's bedroom in the morning. "C'mon, get up and get coffee. I'm dying here!"

Daphne heard rustling on the other end of the phone and could imagine the scene. Kav would be rolling out of bed, throwing on their purple fuzzy robe, and then padding out to the kitchen to get the cup of coffee Bryan made for them before he left for work. It was a very sweet routine they'd gotten into whenever Bryan came to visit during his doctorate program.

Sure enough, a few seconds later, she heard the sound of Kav blowing on their coffee. They sighed. "Now, what did you do? And why do I have a feeling it has to do with Cade and that big old crush you're already developing on him?"

She opened her mouth to say it was rude to think it was about Cade, but realized that was silly. After all, it was, so she just blurted it out. "I. Um. I asked him out? At least I think I did."

"Has he even finished moving in yet?"

"He's moved in. Sort of. He hasn't exactly… unpacked yet." She cringed at her impulsivity.

"Damn, that was fast. And what do you mean 'you think' you asked him out? Did he not hear you?"

"No, he heard me. But, uh, I kind of invited him to dinner, not as a date unless he wanted it to be. And then ran away."

Kav muttered something that sounded suspiciously like "I'm not nearly caffeinated enough for this."

"What?"

"I take it he didn't come after you to answer?"

"No, no he did not. So, you'll have to tell Bryan I'm sorry if I chased off his new employee by having terrible feelings."

"Well, hang on, there. Did he leave? Did he say anything to say it wouldn't be welcome?"

"Well…no. And we *were* cracking flirty jokes in his bed right before."

"His bed, huh? That was fast. Then again, he did ask Bryan if you were single the other night when they were taking the ladder out."

Daphne blinked. "He did? Why didn't you tell me?"

"Because I didn't want you to focus on it like I know

51

you're about to. Anyway, he couldn't take his eyes off you during dinner. Surely you noticed."

"Ugh. You know me too well." She flopped back on her bed. "I need someone to vent to who hasn't known me since I was seven."

Kav snorted. "Sure you do. Did you want advice or just to vent?"

Daphne thought about it. "I think both. Both is good."

"Give him some time to get his bearings and unpack his shit. Then just… enjoy your dinner and see where it goes. Figure out if it feels like a date when you get there."

"That's all well and good for dinner, but there's *so many* hours between now and then. What do I do now?"

"Well, you run your own business, but I do your accounting. If you really can't think of anything to keep you busy, you can work on your receipts."

She gasped with mock horror. "You insinuate my accounting isn't entirely organized? My feelings are hurt!"

"They weren't last month! I'm gonna go shower now. Love you."

"Love you too," Daphne grumbled. She set the phone down on her nightstand and took a deep breath to help her figure out what she needed to do next.

The scent of sweat filled her nose and she knew—she needed to get clean, too.

She made her way to the bathroom, stripped out of her sweaty clothes and started the hot water.

Finally alone in the spray, she let her hands creep down her body as she got all of the hot and bothered energy out with just her quick fingers and overactive imagination.

Then she got to work lathering herself with her favorite lavender and rosemary bath products. By the time she was done, she felt—and smelled—much more like her usual self.

And when she got back to her room, her phone screen was lit up with a message from Giant Man.

"Let's make it a date. You pick the place, I'll pay."

She clutched the phone to her chest and tried to hold in the squeal of delight. She knew exactly where to take him.

six

· · ·

A few hours later, Daphne had finished wrangling her receipt tracking system and she needed to get ready for their date. A quick perusal of her closet had her pulling out a pink and black bra and a jumpsuit she'd been wanting to wear.

It was a deep maroon with cutouts down the front and the sides of her legs, each outlined with something shimmery and gold. It was maybe a little much for a dinner that would be made up of bar snacks, she thought, but then she remembered she was a little much, too. If this was to be a date, he should learn that quickly.

All she needed to complete the look were a few swipes of mascara, eyeliner, and her favorite pink lip gloss.

She stopped at the top of the stairs and peered into the living room. Cade was sitting in her favorite spot on the couch and petting Sushi in her decidedly ridiculous choice of seat—his shoulder.

He looked up at the sound of the creaky stair under her foot and his eyes widened. "You look great," he blurted, then blushed.

It made her body warm with pleasure. She couldn't resist the smile that spread across her face. "Thank you. You ready to roll?"

His gaze went to the cat on his shoulder, as if asking for permission: Sushi chirped and headbutted him in response, doing her best parrot impression. Little weirdo.

Daphne led him out the front door, closing and locking it behind her, then to her car.

Now he was staring at her again, but she didn't think it had anything to do with her outfit this time. He looked distinctly concerned when his eyes met hers across the top of her mint green Volkswagen Beetle. She had no idea why.

"What's the problem? Color not work for you?"

"Daphne, I don't think I'm going to fit in your car. This thing is *small*."

He was right. The top of the car didn't even come up to his shoulders.

"It's bigger than it seems. I know I'm shorter than your gargantuan six foot four, but Bryan fits just fine."

He raised his eyebrows when he replied. "Bryan is also the width of a string bean. This car is tiny!"

He was right about that, too. He probably weighed twice what Bryan did, despite their similar heights, but she had faith in her little car. "I fit perfectly, thank you very much," she told him loftily. "Give it a shot. If you don't fit or you're uncomfortable, we'll take your car or walk. It's only two blocks."

He opened the car door and pushed the seat as far back as it would go. With a dubious look and surprising flexibility, he began to twist himself into the seat. It took him a few minutes and Daphne thought his knees might have been touching his ears, but he got himself buckled.

"I gotta say, Giant Man, I'm impressed at how flexible you are. Are you comfortable enough to get to the bar or do you want to switch cars?"

"Yeah, well, I'm very goal-oriented. And right now, extremely hungry. Let's go."

"Goal-oriented, huh? I'll have to keep that in mind." The words fell out of her mouth before she could stop them, with all the lasciviousness she had been trying to hold back. "Let's get you fed."

She slid into the driver's seat and turned the car on in one smooth movement. Backing down the driveway with ease, she looked at Cade and burst out laughing. He looked as disgruntled and uncomfortable as Sushi did when she crated her to go to the vet. "Are you sure you don't want to switch cars? I don't mind."

He just flapped a hand at the road in front of them, so she drove on.

"Did Bryan and Kav take you this way when they gave you the tour?" she asked after a moment.

"Not yet. They took me down Main Street very briefly, and I tried Weathervane, but that's about all I've had time for."

"Ah, well, there isn't much on this street, but The Mysterious is one of my favorite places."

There wasn't time for much more conversation. Besides, Daphne didn't want to ruin the surprise if she didn't have to. The bar was really better the first time as a surprise.

Sure enough, she watched out of the corner of her eye as his face shifted into astonishment when she pulled into the small but full parking lot.

As they walked in, he got a better look and his expression turned gobsmacked.

"Whoa."

His reaction was exactly the reason she hadn't told him more about it. There was a reason the bar was named The Mysterious. It took kitschiness to an extreme with its occult themes. She loved it.

One wall was almost tiled with different versions of the major arcana. Another wall held a huge illustrated guide to the art of palmistry.

The only 'normal' thing about the bar was its plain wooden bar tables and booths, and even those were decorated with crystal balls and tea cups with tea leaves encapsulated in resin in the bottom.

"This place is… magical," Cade whispered.

"And they've got a decent drink selection. The real reason I brought you here, though, was the snack menu. They make amazing scallion pancakes that are out of this world. Van, can you get an order of those going for me, and a menu for my friend here?"

She waved down the bartender, a white man who would have been her exact height except for his mesy strawberry blond hair, and he handed her two paper menus before heading back to the bar.

She handed one to Cade. He blinked at the menu, then read the offerings out loud to her. "Scallion pancakes with soy ginger dip, french toast grilled cheese with a bloody mary soup, fried pickles with a spicy aioli, spicy apricot chicken wings and gouda? This place is way fancier than I expected."

"It's the best. Know what you want?" Without waiting for an answer, she stood up and raised her voice. "Hey, Van! This is Cade. He's new in town, helping Bryan get the business started."

"Ah, you're the miracle worker! Welcome to Clover

Hill and The Mysterious!" the man called back, starting to make his way back to them. Cade looked at the table in what might have been embarrassment at Van's words but said *Thank you* anyway. "Let me know what you want and I'll get the rest started for you."

Cade studied the menu for a few seconds then said, "Can I get one of everything, actually? I'm really hungry."

Van grinned at him. "A man after my own heart. Can I offer you a drink while you wait?"

That was when Daphne chimed in. She ordered herself a gin and tonic, a glass of water, another order of pancakes and the grilled cheese.

Van raised an eyebrow at her and she stuck her tongue out at him.

"Can I get a whiskey sour?" Cade asked.

"We don't do foam here, that okay?" Van asked. Cade nodded with a relieved expression, and Van just laughed. Daphne wasn't sure what that was about, but she didn't really care.

Daphne led them back to her favorite bar table, where she settled onto her stool with a sigh of contentment. The stools were large enough to be comfortable for her wide hips, which was rare.

She was beginning to love watching him in this new place, seeing the wonder and joy on his face. It was refreshing to spend time with someone who didn't seem to have a cynical bone in his body. His very attractive body.

Moments later, Van arrived with their drinks and the first part of their food order. Cade's eyes locked onto the plate and widened at the sight of the scallion pancakes.

"These look amazing. Why the folded shape, though?"

"So they can have more sauce on them! The pockets make it perfect." Daphne grabbed one and broke it open so that the scent of scallions and spices filled the air between them. Cade took a deep breath in, then smiled.

"It smells amazing. Mind if I take one, since this is technically yours?"

She took a bite and pretended to think about it just long enough for his hopeful expression—and extended hand—to falter.

"Yeah, go for it. I'll just steal some of yours when they get here."

His fingers grabbed a pancake so quickly she barely saw them move, but she saw when he took his first bite. His eyes widened.

"This is delicious. Is all the food this good?"

"You have no idea."

As they ate, they talked about the things people would generally learn about each other *before* they moved in together. "So, what made you choose physical therapy?"

"I was in all kinds of sports as a kid. Anything they let me play, I was on the team. So, it stands to reason I also got injured fairly regularly," he explained. "My mom joked I'd spent so much time in PT by the time I graduated high school that I basically had an honorary degree in it. When I thought about what I wanted to do after school, it just seemed natural to give this a shot. And it turned out I liked it, so here I am. How about you?"

"I like being in charge of things and I like spending time with people," Daphne laughed. "Event planning just seemed natural, and I really enjoy it. Even when things get complicated or you've got a pain-in-the-ass client, like my last one at my previous job."

Van chose that moment to drop off a few more plates of mouth-watering food.

"Oh. My. God. This is the best place ever," he groaned as he dug in.

"I know, right? Just wait 'til you actually eat the rest of it."

He didn't need any further encouragement, and neither did she. They made quick work of all of it, then ordered more of the french toast grilled cheese for him and scallion pancakes for her.

"Like, today, I got to meet with some pretty cool kids who are getting married," she said around bites of the pancakes folded up like fortune cookies. "Well, I say kids, but they're both nineteen. Not my friends who are getting married—we went to school together so we're all in our late thirties. Amber and Hari are just a lot younger than me. That's the hard part about this job."

"Being around young people?" He sounded skeptical, and she laughed.

"No, being around people who are just... almost nause-atingly in love, you know? These two have been in love for basically their whole lives. It can be hard not to get jealous sometimes."

"If love is what you're searching for, you'll find it. I believe in you." The words were so solemn she had to take a drink to steady herself.

"Well, we'll see about that," she replied, then hastily changed the subject. "Anyway, did I tell you? The other thing I love about this bar is the pool table. Spike's doesn't have one, and I am an excellent pool hustler. I got a good chunk of my Mint to Be startup funds making bets on my pool game on work trips. Used to drive my ex up the wall. You want to try your luck?"

Cade took a sip of his drink before he answered.

"Believe it or not, I've never actually played. Is it hard to learn?"

Daphne sat up a little straighter on her stool. "Not at all! In fact, I could teach you now if you want?"

"That'd be great!" Cade moved so quickly to stand up that he nearly fell off his chair. Daphne grabbed his arm to keep it from hitting the bar as he caught himself with the other.

"Easy there, Giant Man," she teased. "You sure you're not too drunk to learn a new game that requires coordination?"

He just smiled up at her with his hair flopping into his eyes. The sight made her heart squeeze. Suddenly, she wasn't sure whether touching him was the best idea she'd ever had or the worst. Either way, she didn't want to let go of his muscular arm.

The only reason she could think to hang onto him was to lead him over to the pool table in the back room. It was only a few steps, but it was better than nothing.

"Okay, how much do you know about pool?"

"I know there's a stick and you hit the balls into the pockets and… that's about it."

She could work with that. She pulled a pool cue off the wall and handed it to him, then pulled another one off for herself.

"I'm gonna keep it real simple. Now, you're solids, I'm stripes. You want to get your balls into the pockets, leaving the eight ball for last. If you hit one of mine in, it counts as my point."

"Like in soccer?"

Daphne shrugged. "I am not super familiar with soccer, so I'll go with yes. If you hit your ball into the pocket, you get another shot. If you hit the cue ball off the table or into one of the pockets, that's called a scratch. I think in sports terms it would be like a foul? Anyway, if you scratch, you forfeit your turn. I get to pick up the cue ball, put it wherever I want and shoot. And if that happens, I will win. So try not to do it," she said cheekily.

That made him laugh. They were still standing so close together she could feel the rumble in his chest against her own. It sent the butterflies she'd been holding in all night back to fluttering.

He pulled away from her and lined up his shot. She couldn't take her eyes off the line of his body when he flexed his muscles and hit the ball.

She could tell by how much force he put into the strike that it was going to scratch. And it scratched magnificently —bouncing off the table's wall, then a ball and then onto the hardwood floor with a loud thud.

Daphne didn't bother to stifle her laugh. "That... is an excellent example of a scratch. We'll call that a first try and—"

Van's voice called from the doorway, as if he'd been waiting for a loud noise. "Oy in there! You break one of my balls, you buy me a whole new set."

A snort-laugh burst out of Cade before he covered his face with one large hand. "Sorry, Van! I'll be more careful with the next shot, I promise."

She could hear Van chuckling as he walked back to the bar.

"Anyway, we'll call that a first shot. I'll give you a second one, just this once. After that, I'm taking all your money."

He snort-laughed again. She was beginning to love that sound.

He lined up his shot for the second time, and this time

she watched his hands instead of his ass. Now she saw the reason he had scratched. He was holding the cue all wrong and putting too much force into it.

She grabbed his arm, relishing the way her fingers tingled as they planted themselves into his muscle. "Whoa, hold on there, Giant Man. You're getting ready to do the same thing again. Here, let me show you."

She let her hand slide down his rippling arm until she nearly held his right hand. With gentle fingers, she guided it into a more suitable position near the base of the cue. Then she reached around his front, wrapping her other hand around his left hand to move his fingers into a shape that would help him guide his shots more evenly.

"This should be more comfortable for you, and help you avoid bouncing off the table."

His eyes were not on his hands at all. They were on her boobs, which were very in his face thanks to the position she'd unthinkingly put herself in.

Heat flushed from the tips of her ears all the way down her body as he stared at her with attraction plain on his face. If anyone else was looking at her like that, she'd be beating a hasty retreat and possibly that person. But when he tried to pull his eyes up to meet hers, they snagged on her mouth.

She bit her lip as she smiled, and was rewarded by hearing the large man in front of her suck in a breath and try to take a step back.

For the second time that night, he tripped and nearly fell. This time, it was her turn to catch him with her body. Thanks to their awkward position, they fell into the pool table. She wasn't sure how, but somehow in the tussle she wound up with her back over the table with his body bent over hers, only held up by the strong arms that bracketed her torso. They both breathed heavily as they looked at each other, and Daphne was fairly sure it wasn't just from the shock of the fall.

"You know, if you wanted to kiss me, you didn't have to go through the trouble of bowling me over. You could have just asked," she breathed.

He smiled, but his eyes were serious and sober as he looked into hers. "Can I kiss you?"

Her answer was to push herself up against him using the tangle of their legs until there was only a breath between them. He pressed his lips to hers in a kiss that was no less searing for its gentleness. She kissed him back more forcefully and he accepted her lead. With every stroke of his tongue, they pulled each other closer until there was nothing between them but their clothes. And even those were in danger of coming off if they didn't take a break.

Cade was the one that broke the kiss, but he didn't pull away any further than he had to. When he spoke, his lips still brushed hers. "I swear I'm much better with my hands than my performance here tonight shows. Will you let me show you?"

How could she resist that invitation? She couldn't wait to get her hands on him in private.

Somehow, they made it out of the car, up the stairs, and into Daphne's bedroom without either separating or tripping on anything even though neither of them could tear their gaze away from the other. Cade was pretty sure that was a minor miracle, and he was thanking God.

They tumbled into her bed, their hands all over each

other. She'd already unbuttoned half his shirt. He wanted to see more of her, all of her. Cade kissed his way down her neck and shoulder, savoring the taste of her, but when he tried to slide the strap of her jumpsuit off, it wouldn't move.

The fabric had a bit of stretch, but it wasn't stretchy enough to just pull off her shoulders. Despite her allowing him to run his hands up and down her back, he couldn't find a closure of any kind.

"This jumpsuit is beautiful. But how the hell do I get it off you?" he growled.

She laughed, a deep, throaty sound that made Cade growl for an entirely different reason. Then she shifted her arm to curl into her armpit, thrusting her chest into his face. With one swift movement, she pulled the side zipper down to reveal her beautifully pale skin.

Right. It had been so long since he'd worn something that required a hidden zipper, he had forgotten those were a thing. He could take it from here, though.

The more he got her undressed, the more he loved her body. He slowly uncovered her bra and panties—a matched set of bright pink cotton with a hint of black lace around the leg—making sure to taste and explore as much of her as he could. When he had freed her of both and was taking the time to admire every roll and stretch mark, she took back over, moving them so she was on top of him.

"You're wearing too many clothes," she grumbled. "Take 'em off."

"Yes, ma'am," he agreed.

Her eyes, then her hands, traced his body as he lifted the undershirt over his head. She unbuckled his belt for him and shoved his jeans and briefs down in one smooth movement. As he kicked them off, she sucked in a breath.

The freedom, and her clear admiration of his body, made his pussy clench and his cock ache.

"Can I touch you?"

"God, please." The words burst out of him with a raw edge to his voice.

Her hands started at his shoulders and slid down his pecs and belly and lower until she wrapped her fingers around his small cock. Her touch felt like lightning on the testosterone-enlarged bundle of nerves and he never wanted it to stop.

Luck was on his side tonight, because she didn't. She teased and pressed at his cock until his orgasm coursed through him.

Then it was his turn to flip her onto her back and continue mapping her voluptuous body with his mouth and hands. When he reached her hips, he looked up at her, wanting permission.

He found her holding out a dental dam packet. Without wondering where she'd pulled it from or how he hadn't noticed, he opened it and laid it across her pussy with fingers that shook slightly. She shivered at his touch, so he laid a kiss on each corner. With pleasure, Cade traced his way around her outer lips, making his way slowly inward until he reached her entrance.

Her natural aroma of musk and salt mixed with the latex and filled his senses until she was all he could imagine.

Her moans and heavy breathing were the only sounds he cared about. They got louder and her back arched as he found a rhythm she liked and did more of it. He couldn't get enough of her, and it seemed like it was mutual.

As her pussy ground against his face, her curly blonde hair tangled with his beard. It was like their bodies were doing everything they could to avoid being separated for even an instant, and he was glad for it. He just wished he could taste her, to see if she tasted as good as she felt underneath his mouth, but it didn't matter when she came apart on his tongue.

In that moment, she was his whole world. And then something heavy and sharp attached itself to his head.

He reeled back with a bellow, and the pain intensified. "What the fuck?"

The attacker replied with an ear-splitting yowl and they both realized what was happening. It was the cat.

"Sushi! No! Let go of him!" Daphne's *oh* face had turned into an *oh shit* face, even as she reached for the cat. Daphne's hands were met with more yowling and the release of one paw from his scalp to swipe at her owner.

He tried to move his head to shake her off, but her claws dug into his hair and scalp.

"No ma'am!" Both Cade and the cat stilled at the sound of her suddenly stern voice. The next thing he knew, she was throwing clothes at his face, and the white hot pain in his skull became much less sharp.

Then he heard the skitter of cat claws running away from him very quickly and Daphne was on her knees on the edge of the bed.

"I am so sorry, oh my god. I had no idea that was even... are you okay? Let me look at your head!" She pulled his head toward her without waiting for permission and sucked in a breath. She touched a finger to where most of the pain was located and he felt something squish.

He pulled back with a hiss, only for her to apologize again, but she still didn't let go of his head. "You're in luck, sort of. I don't think you're gonna need stitches. You are going to need to clean these, though. No matter how clean she thinks her claws are, I am positive these will get infected if you don't. Come with me."

She punctuated the end of her request with a gentle kiss to an uninjured part of the top of his head. It somehow made him feel better and more confused at the same time.

"You don't need to apologize," he told her as he pulled himself up from his knees. "It's not like you ordered the cat to attack me, right?"

"No, no I didn't. I didn't even think about how she might react to me having sex. I haven't needed to. But she's still my responsibility, so, I'm sorry."

"Just help me clean up and we'll be even stevens."

She smiled. Neither of them bothered to get dressed before they stumbled to her hallway bathroom.

Her bathroom was much larger than the one attached to his, and much more personalized. Like the rest of the house, it was meticulously decorated. Unlike the rest of the house, it was decorated with framed, artistic nude pictures of people of all genders, races and sizes. They were all in different art styles, some sketched with charcoal, some painted with oil or acrylic.

When he looked in the mirror and saw them reflected back at him alongside their two naked bodies, it felt like he was looking at a painting. It was beautiful. *They* were beautiful.

His view was restricted when she opened the cabinet and pulled out a tube of antibiotic cream. Her hands and expression were gentle as she worked the cream into his scalp.

"You have really beautiful hair, you know. It's a shame I'm only touching it because my cat is an absolute asshole."

That made him laugh, and he made eye contact with her in the mirror for the first time. "Thank you. I take it that's never happened before?"

She shook her head vigorously, and his eyes were caught as the rest of her body almost shimmied with the movement. "No, she has never been the least bit aggressive with anything but her squeaky toys. Of course, I also haven't given her much opportunity to experience this particular situation."

"Not much for bringing dates home?" Her mouth twisted as soon as the words came out, and he could tell he'd hit on a sore spot. "Sorry, you don't have to answer."

"Just a lack of opportunity. Sushi was a gift from my parents, in the hope she would help me cheer up after my last breakup. It was a rough one, partially because it also coincided with me being fired."

"You got fired right after your breakup? That's really shitty timing. I'm sorry."

Her fingers stilled in his hair. He'd said something wrong for sure, but he didn't know what it was, so he just repeated the apology. She looked up at him in the mirror, biting the lips he'd been kissing just a few minutes ago, then gave a forced smile.

Her voice was quieter now than it had been. "I knew it was coming. It's what happens when you date your boss's daughter and things go south."

Oh. That explained it. "That still really sucks. Did the cat help?"

"She really did. At least, until tonight. She has terrible timing for learning new tricks."

He couldn't disagree on that point. "Well, at least she waited until we had both gotten off once." This made Daphne smile a little, so he continued. "It may not have been quite the slow seduction I had hoped for, but... maybe next time?"

Now her smile reached her eyes as she pulled her hands free of his hair. "Next time, we'll shut the door and take all the time we want. Just say the word. But for now, I need to go check on Sushi and make sure she's not traumatized. She's still pretty young, after all."

"Of course! Should I come, too? I don't want her to think I'm mad at her."

Daphne stepped away from him and shook her head. "I've got this handled. Thanks, though."

He watched her go, gathered his clothing from the bedroom floor, then went back to his own room to clean up. This was not at all what he expected the end of this evening to be. It wasn't exactly an unqualified success, but it hadn't been bad either. Despite the pain in his head, he couldn't help thinking it had been a good night. As he drifted off to sleep, he hoped 'next time' wouldn't be too far away.

seven

. . .

Daphne woke the next morning two minutes before her 6:15 alarm, like always.

Something felt different today, though, and she couldn't quite put her finger on it until she looked at her phone. Then she realized what was missing. Sushi.

Every morning for the last four months, Sushi had sat on the nightstand and waited for Daphne to wake up and feed her. Except, this morning, she wasn't there. Or on the pillow on the other side of the bed where she often liked to sleep. Something was wrong.

Daphne flung off her blankets. If the cat wasn't in any of her usual places, that meant Trouble with a capital T.

She looked in the closet and hampers first, then under the bed and dresser, making her way around the room with eagle eyes. She couldn't find the gray beast anywhere. Her next stop was the bathroom, then down the stairs to see if she was waiting somewhere there, instead. But the living room and kitchen were entirely cat-free. Daphne was very definitely freaking out.

All the doors and windows were closed, so she couldn't have gotten out, she reminded herself. *Where haven't you looked?*

She named each room she'd been in, counting them off on her fingers until she'd gotten through every room in the house but one.

Cade's room.

With a groan, she made herself go back upstairs. Sure enough, his door was open just wide enough for a trouble-some kitten to get through. She moved to poke her head in, then stopped herself. They may have slept together, but she didn't have permission to just walk into his space while he slept.

But, as she stood there, she didn't hear anything inside. No snoring or the shuffles of someone getting ready for their day. Either he was a really quiet sleeper or he wasn't there.

Daphne was sure he would understand the need to find Sushi, but it made her feel weird all the same. Just a quick peek and then she'd get out.

She flipped her phone's flashlight on and took a deep breath before slowly opening the door just far enough for her to fit through. She didn't have to go far to see exactly where her cat had gone. The light filtering through the door showed Sushi curled in a ball directly in the center of the pile of pillows.

Cade *wasn't* there. He must be an early riser, to her surprise, to get up and out before she'd even woken up.

She wondered, briefly, what it would have been like to have spent the rest of the night with him. Would he have woken her before he left, or would he have stayed in bed until her alarm went off?

"Looking for something?"

She whirled around and found Cade standing at the

top of the stairs in a pair of shorts and tank top that showed off *tons* of glistening skin.

"S-Sushi, actually." She pointed to the bed, and he got closer to her so he could see over her shoulder.

He snorted when he spotted the cat. "Clearly she's changed her mind about me since last night."

"Or at least your pillows," Daphne laughed. "Speaking of, how's your head?"

He tilted his head at her and smiled mischievously. "I don't know, got any complaints?"

"No, no complaints." She smacked his chest lightly when he laughed. "I meant the cat scratches, and you know it. Those can go bad very fast if you're not careful."

He stepped back from her and touched his head gingerly, as if he was afraid to press too hard. "Honestly, I'm fine. I'll give them a good scrub once I take a shower to be safe. Which I actually need to do. I can't go to my first day of work looking like this, after all."

She recognized a dismissal when she heard one. "Right. Well, now that I've found the cat, I'm gonna go make some coffee and breakfast. Do you want some?"

"Coffee would be great. But if you wait, I'll help you make breakfast."

"I'll take it. See you in a few."

Cade didn't rush through his shower, but he didn't exactly take his time either.

Soft morning sun lit his bedroom through the window as he got ready for his first day of work.

He pulled the outfit he'd planned for his first day out of his closet and got dressed. Normally, he went to work in joggers and tank tops, but he wanted to be a little bit fancier today. He chose a pair of khakis and a frog-patterned button-down shirt and let his hair curl loosely around his shoulders.

He thought he looked good, but he wasn't sure what Bryan was expecting from him today. He could feel his anxiety building, but some deep breaths and breakfast would go a long way to fixing that.

Grabbing his wallet, keys, and phone, he took the stairs two at a time. He couldn't wait to spend more time with Daphne. He wished he could've spent the night next to her, but it was probably too early for that.

He wasn't exactly sure what their relationship was now, but she *had* mentioned a next time. So she probably didn't just want a one-night stand. He didn't have time to worry about that right this second, though, because he had a breakfast to cook.

She must've heard him coming, because she spoke without turning to look at him.

"I'm thinking omelets with toast. Sound okay to you?"

Looking around the kitchen, he saw that she had gotten out the ingredients, and he nodded. "Sounds good. I'm pretty good with a spatula, so tell me how you like yours and enjoy your coffee."

He was sure she was going to shoot back that she could cook her own omelet, and sure enough, she spun to look at him with her coffee mug in hand. Then she did a double take. "Wow, you look great."

Cade tugged at the bottom of the shirt self-consciously. "It's not too funky for Bryan?"

Daphne looked him up and down before replying. "Just funky enough, I think. He'll probably ask where you got it from so he can get one of his own. Now, if you're going to be cooking breakfast, I'll fix your coffee. Deal?"

They traded preferences—he liked two spoonfuls of sugar and a decent amount of milk in his coffee, and she liked her omelets with mushrooms, bell peppers and cheese. Before long, each of them had a steaming plate in front of them.

"Are you excited to start work?"

He tilted his hand from side to side as he swallowed his coffee. "Right now, I'm more nervous than anything, but I'm looking forward to it. I've never done anything quite like this before."

"Well, I'm sure you'll be great at it," she said firmly.

"I appreciate the confidence, even though you have nothing to base it on other than your new knowledge of my physique," he joked.

She snorted into her coffee. "It is a mighty fine physique, certainly, but I have a little more to go on. Bryan takes his business seriously. He wouldn't have asked for permission to hire you if you hadn't been doing well at his Pop's place. Have faith in him, if you don't have it in yourself."

That was a surprisingly wise statement for this hour of the morning, Cade thought. It made him feel a little bit better as he asked the other question weighing on his mind.

"Speaking of physiques... we should probably talk at some point?"

"That would be smart," Daphne agreed, and relief washed over him. "Let's talk tonight over dinner."

By the time he got into the car with his thermos a few minutes later, his anxiety was becoming a little more like excitement.

He put the address into his GPS app, then laughed because he didn't need to. He could have walked or biked, if he'd left himself enough time. It was maybe five blocks away, on the next street over. He left his phone on his dashboard, just in case, and started to drive.

On one side of the street, he saw Holly's Groceteria, a boba tea shop, and sub shop. On the other, Cade saw the back side of the bakery, the tea shop Daphne had mentioned the previous day, and what he vaguely remembered to be a thrift store before he found the storefront that would be Cracked Up Chiropractic.

The location was good from what he could tell, but it wasn't much to look at yet. The windows had been covered in newspaper from the interior, and the cloth canopy had been removed so there was just a half-circle of metal sticking out from the red brick. He had a feeling it would be something special once they were done with it.

Before he slid his phone and his back pocket, a text from Michael popped up. It was just a simple *you've got this* with the muscle arm emoji.

Between him and Daphne, Cade was starting to feel like maybe he actually did.

Much like the exterior, the interior was a blank canvas. There were five doors leading to small rooms around the exterior of the space. A wall segmented the space in two, creating a front desk area with a hallway and a surprisingly spacious working area.

He guessed it would be enough space for a couple of chiropractic tables and a decently sized physical therapy section. The biggest difference between the outside and inside was that the interior wasn't completely unoccupied. Bryan stood in the back corner next to a folding table with a small smile on his face.

"What do you think? Did I choose all right?" He was bouncing on his toes a little bit and his eyes were sparkling.

Cade took another look at the room, seeing what it could be, and smiled back at his new boss. "Oh yeah, I think you chose just fine. I think you're going to need some stuff, though."

"Then it's mighty convenient I've got a list going and my checkbook ready. A lot of lists, actually. I must admit most of them are from Google, though."

Cade laughed. "Where else would we start? Got a chair for me?"

The other man reached behind him and pulled out a metal folding chair, setting it up next to the table with a flourish. Cade grimaced at the thought of spending all day in a bad chair, but he could deal.

"Real office chairs show up tomorrow at 11, along with a front desk that will give us somewhere to actually work. I wanted to have them today, but you know how shipping can be. For now, we have this table and a lot of hand-written lists."

He wasn't kidding. There were three notebooks on the table in front of them, all open to pages with lists of things the clinic needed.

The list closest to him read *Chiropractic Equipment*, and while the list nearly filled the page, most items were crossed off or had notes saying things like "wait 3mos."

What remained included most of the basic things he had already thought of—chiro tables, traction chairs, sacral blocks, tens units, a theragun, scheduling and record software.

There was something major missing from it, though. An expensive something.

"What are you going to do about x-rays? I know the machinery's pretty expensive on top of everything else you need for start-up costs, but I understand they're important."

Bryan grimaced. "Upwards of fifteen grand expensive. Pop and I were talking about it, and there are options for used machines, or we could go for a leased machine. It might be more expensive in the long run, but it would let us get started with something with a guaranteed repair."

Cade made a thoughtful sound. They were good options, but there was one he hadn't mentioned. "Is there any way you could outsource it?"

Bryan shook his head. "The only place with an x-ray machine within a ten-mile radius is the hospital. It would cause more problems than it solves. Not only would it be a huge wait to process them, it would be way more expensive for my patients. I'd rather spend the money to make things as accessible as possible."

That made sense. "The only other thing you're going to want to add to this list is a very large order of Biofreeze. The stuff is magical, plus, people are willing to buy it for home use. You've got another list for your PT, right?"

Bryan looked at the other notebooks on the table with confusion, then dug into his bag and pulled out three more. He held one out to Cade with a hopeful expression. "Flip through and see if you can find it. I'll take the others."

Cade snorted, but took the notebook. The lists inside

were much like the ones on the table, but less organized, if possible.

Cade was gonna have to find a better system if this was Bryan's usual way of handling lists. There was nothing in the notebook about physical therapy equipment, but before he could say anything, Bryan made a joyful noise.

"Found it. I only remember the things I've used personally, so please let me know if I forgot something."

This list was much shorter than the previous, simply listing exercise balls, yoga mats, and weights. Here was a way he could be useful. "This is a good start, but you're gonna need way more stuff for even a basic physical therapy set up. Some of the fancier stuff can wait until you're a little more established, or you have a client who needs it. I assume you're trying to reduce up-front spending?"

When Bryan nodded, Cade grabbed a pen and added low-weight dumbbells, cuff weights, resistance bands, medicine balls, foam rolls, and wall bars to the list.

"Okay, now we've got that settled, let's talk a little bit about what your timeline looks like. You mentioned on the phone you'd like to do a soft opening next month, right?"

"Yeah. I know it'll be a tight turnaround with getting everything here, but the big stuff is already on its way, and we'd like to start doing interviews next week. I think we can do it, between the two of us. Right?"

Cade looked around the empty building until his eyes rested on the many lists in front of him. His heart thumped nervously, but he smiled back at his new boss. "Yeah, I think we can. Let's get to work."

Daphne walked in the door that evening feeling like a pack mule with all the food she'd ordered from Dragon Palace.

She'd texted Cade around lunch to ask what he typically ordered from Chinese restaurants, but had gotten no reply. He had told her the other day he would eat almost anything, but she hadn't wanted to order something he hated.

Inspiration struck as she ran her finger down the menu and realized she didn't know what she wanted, either. None of her go-to favorites were screaming for her to pick them. That didn't mean she couldn't get them, though.

She had ordered a range of the smaller versions of their entrees, plus an order of egg rolls and crab rangoons. She'd even eaten a few of the rangoons to tide her over on her way home. Everybody liked those. And, as always, the restaurant had thrown in some freebies that smelled amazing.

Now, she just had to figure out how to make the words in her brain come out correctly before he got home in roughly fifteen minutes. No pressure.

Sushi chose that moment to hop up on the kitchen table and yell at her, as if to say she was being silly. She probably was. After all, she barely knew him and it wasn't like they could have a long-term future together with the way things stood. He would be leaving in three months and going back to his real life.

It didn't stop her from wanting to learn everything she could about him in the meantime. She could only hope he felt the same way.

Cade's nerves picked up as he walked into the house. He called out a greeting, but didn't see Daphne when he looked around. Instead, Sushi used her claws to climb up his body so she could sit on his shoulder. He was going to have to talk to Daphne about it. They had to do something about those claws before she got them into something a little more tender than just his thighs.

Speaking of Daphne, she had come through with her promise of dinner. He couldn't pin down exactly what it was, but it smelled delicious. She couldn't remember the last time he'd come home to a meal someone else had done all the work for.

When he walked into the kitchen and saw her standing next to the table—now completely absent of signs of their light accident a few days prior—he realized why he couldn't tell what was there. She'd ordered what looked like the entire menu from someplace called Dragon Palace. How many people was she trying to feed?

Cade tried to count the takeout boxes, but kept getting distracted by the cat purring in his ear. Finally, he gave up and just asked. "Are we having company for dinner?"

She tilted her head at him. "No? It's just us. We said we were going to talk about our relationship or the possibility of one. Why would I invite other people over?"

"I—I just meant, there's a surprising amount of food on the table. I know I eat a lot, but it seems like too much for two people."

She waved her hand at him. "Of course it is. I wasn't sure what you liked and you weren't answering your phone, so I got a little bit of everything I liked and a couple new things. Whatever neither of us likes can go to Bryan and Kav, and everything else will make a couple good leftover meals."

His phone? He hadn't heard it go off since he'd walked into Cracked Up Chiropractic. That was weird, now that he thought about it. He patted his pockets until he found his lifeline to the outside world.

Which was dead.

"Crap, I must have forgotten to charge it last night after..." He blushed. "I'm sorry. I'll be more careful from now on."

"With charging your phone? Or with me?"

He wasn't sure how to answer. "Both? I think?"

"Um, do you want to eat first? Or should we just get it out since we're already sort of talking about it?"

That made him smile. "Let's just get it out there. Secrets and nerves are bad for digestion. If that's okay with you, of course."

She smiled at him, but there was something nervous about it. "So I wanted to know if you were interested in having a relationship, or if you just wanted to be friends with benefits, or if you just wanted a one-night stand. No judgment on what you're thinking, I just think we need to get onto the same page." She took a deep breath and continued. "I think you and I might make a really great couple if we gave it time. It's unusual for me to sleep with someone before I've really gotten to know them, but there's something between us that really makes me want to know more. That is, if you're interested."

Every word bloomed in his chest like a flower in the sun. For once, he knew exactly what he wanted to say. "Daphne, I have been interested in you since the moment you fell into my arms. I don't ever want you to be confused about that. You are brilliant and commanding and beautiful, and our night together might have been unplanned, but I wouldn't trade it for anything. Well, except maybe the abrupt ending."

She laughed shakily.

Cade hoped his smile was reassuring as he continued. "I know I'm not supposed to stay in Clover Hill after August, and that makes things complicated, but... I think we could have some fun for now and figure out the rest later. What do you think?"

"I think that sounds nice, even if it scares me a little. I'm not... I don't like not having a plan."

He reached out to her and she fitted herself against him.

"It scares me, too," Cade admitted. "But you're like, really smart and I'm very flexible. I think we can figure it out together while we're here. Don't you think?"

Now she smiled at him, and he was unable to resist his urge to pull her closer and kiss her trembling lips. She tasted of chili sauce, cream cheese and something else he couldn't quite identify. He couldn't get enough.

Eventually, though, they had to break apart to breathe. Daphne grinned.

"What do you say we go have some of that fun now? The food will hold."

That was the best idea he'd heard all day.

eight

. . .

Daphne threw her car into park and climbed out almost before the Bug finished rocking. She can't believe how late she'd let her meeting with Amber and Hari go.

They were lovely women and she'd been having so much fun she hadn't even looked at her phone until her alarm had gone off to remind her to leave. She was sure she had made quite the impression as she scrambled to get out of there.

She dashed inside and up the stairs, noticing the music playing but not stopping to listen. Cade was home. That would make things easier.

She still had to change, pack her bag, and make sure Cade had everything he needed for the weekend. At this point, she was going to be pushing the line of late for the last meeting with Rook and Lily's hotel's wedding coordinator. That left very little time for the goodbye she had been craving all day, which she hated. She also had to rush, which she hated even more.

Maybe if she hustled, she could make it just a little longer. Undressing with a speed she hadn't known she had, she slid into a royal blue dress that always made her feel great. That would help her feel less stressed about the time. She ran through the list of things she'd need and packed them, other than her wedding planning binder. Which… she didn't see anywhere.

Maybe she had left it in the living room. She grabbed her suitcase and ran downstairs, not caring how much noise she made as she hunted for it. But there was no sign of it in any of her usual places, even in the couch cushions, and she was starting to panic.

The bright red binder that held all her notes, plans, and contingencies for the wedding she was in charge of. She absolutely had to have it to do her job properly, and if it wasn't here…

Maybe the kitchen? She had been going over the plans with Kav during lunch. Maybe she had left it in with the weekly flyers from local businesses and other mail that she hadn't dealt with yet.

She walked into the adjoining room, expecting to see the mess she had left a few hours before. Instead, the room was so clean it nearly sparkled. There were even fresh flowers in the window above the sink.

Daphne was no slouch when it came to housework, but the room in front of her could have been something out of a magazine spread, if not for the giant man standing next to the sink chopping vegetables and singing along to his music.

"Oh, wow."

Cade nearly jumped out of his skin as he spun toward her with the knife raised. Daphne put her hands in the air while she tried—and failed—to keep herself from laughing.

He lowered the knife as he realized who had spoken.

"Jesus Christ, you scared me! You can't sneak up on a man with a knife like that!"

That made her laugh even harder. "I don't think you can call it sneaking when I've been in the house for fifteen minutes. You didn't hear me come in or any of the noise I made while I was rummaging around the living room?"

Now he laughed with her. "I really didn't! Why were you rummaging around in the living room? That was next on my cleaning list."

"I'm looking for my binder for this wedding. It's red and it's got all my notes and contracts and everything in it. Did you see it when you cleaned?"

He looked around the room with a frown. "I didn't. All I saw were some flyers for Holly's Groceteria and some box stores. I thought it was here last night for dinner, though."

She grimaced. "I thought so, too. But Kav was here earlier for lunch and to get their mail and now I don't know where I put it—oh. Kav was here. Maybe they know where I put it."

She whipped out her phone and dialed her best friend, hoping beyond hope they would answer.

It was Bryan's baritone voice coming through the speaker before she could say anything, though. "Hey, have you left yet? I was about to call you. Kav is on their way over there now but left the phone here. They accidentally grabbed your wedding binder and just realized it."

Oh, thank fuck. Judging by Cade's snort, she'd said that out loud. She cleared her throat, trying not to be embarrassed. "Thanks for letting me know, Bryan. I'll see you tomorrow for the rehearsal dinner, right?"

"Yep, we'll be there—early to help you with whatever you need."

"You're the best! See you then!" She barely heard his reply as she ended the call. If Kav had already left, she had fifteen minutes max to pack her car and say her goodbyes. That was way more time than she had planned on taking, but it was out of her control. She and her therapist had done a lot of work over the last few years so she could handle situations like this without panicking.

She took a deep breath and turned to Cade. "Can you help me bring all of my things to the car?"

He smiled softly at her. "Of course, Daphne. Lead the way."

Cade could see Daphne freaking out. He could also see she was working hard to bring herself back to normal while they packed the car. She hadn't really needed his help with her suitcase and purse, but he was glad to take a little bit off her shoulders.

She reminded him of where Sushi's food was and when she was to be fed.

"Oh, I wish I had my binder already," she lamented. "I've got a copy of my itinerary for you in there so you'll know when I'm available to return calls. Hopefully nothing will go wrong, but if it does, you've got my number."

"Why don't you tell me the general schedule and I'll put it in my phone?" he offered. He had never been particularly good at keeping track of paperwork.

She blinked at him, as if the idea surprised her. Then she did something to surprise him back—flung her arms around his neck with so much force his back pressed against the car, and kissed him with passion.

A triumphant-sounding laugh startled them into taking a breath. "I knew it! I knew something was going on there! The best-friend psychic bond is correct once more!"

Cade looked up to find Kav nearly hanging out of their car window as they parked. He knew he should be embarrassed, but he couldn't find the energy. He was just sad when Daphne stepped away from him.

"Mind your own business, Kav. Or else I'll tell Cade about the time I caught you and Bryan in flagrante right here on the porch swing. And quit stealing my binders! You know I can't function without them!"

"Why do you think I hauled ass to get this to you before you left?" They ducked back into their SUV. When they re-emerged, they held a binder that very nearly matched the car's paint job.

Daphne nearly sprinted to snatch it from them, then back to where he stood.

"Thank you so much, I'll see you tomorrow for the rehearsal dinner. I have to leave now, though. Cade—send me pictures of Sushi throughout the weekend, please?"

He smiled and pressed a kiss to her cheek. "Of course. As many as you want."

She pulled a piece of paper from the binder and thrust it into his hand. "I'll call you tomorrow, okay? I really have to go now, though."

He was already looking forward to it. "Drive safely!"

Without another word, she climbed into her tiny car and backed out of the driveway, waving at him and Kav both before driving toward the sun.

When her car disappeared around the corner, Kav called him over to them. "I'm not going to do the *if you hurt her* song and dance. You two are adults and I'm not about to get in the way of your fun. I just wanted to ask you to be careful with her. She puts up a good front, but she's less guarded than she pretends to be."

Cade couldn't help but smile. Even though he was a full foot taller than Kav and more than double their weight, he had no doubt they could hurt him.

"I will keep that in mind," he said solemnly. "I'll do everything in my power to keep from hurting her. You have my word."

"Good. Then I'm off to call and rag on her for keeping you a secret." They grinned wolfishly. "Take care of Sushi. That's her baby."

"I'll do my best!"

Warning given, Kav gave him a wave and drove off. He made his way inside, glad Daphne had friends so willing to look out for her. He knew that, if they were in his town, Michael would have given Daphne the same warning.

When he finally looked at the itinerary she'd handed him, he was amazed. She had *a lot* packed into three days —a wedding party brunch tomorrow morning, the rehearsal dinner that evening, and then the wedding on Saturday. Daphne planned to return home on Sunday morning, which made sense to him. He would have been exhausted by just attending all of them, let alone working them all.

Cade resolved to make sure nothing went wrong while she was gone. He was going to make sure that everything at home was taken care of, and have a nice lunch ready when she got home. It would be just the thing.

Daphne knew the instant Kav got home, because her phone began to ring. She took her hand off the wheel to pinch the bridge of her nose and sighed before answering.

Kav's voice warbled out of the speakers, to the tune of "Tradition" from *Fiddler on the Roof*. "I knew it, I knew it, I knew it, I knew it!"

"I will hang up this phone if you don't stop," she warned. Kav laughed, marking the blessed end of the terrible singing. "Now, do you want to brag about how right you were or do you want the details? Because I would desperately love to think about something other than how late I'm going to be to this meeting."

"Details please!" they answered, as she'd known they would.

nine

. . .

Cade woke from the best dream of his life, one where Daphne had been bouncing on his strap-on with abandon, calling his name as she came.

His reality was a lot less fun. The only pounding going on here was on the door, and he knew it wasn't his girlfriend.

He rolled out of bed, grabbing and sliding into the pair of sweatpants he always kept handy in case of emergencies.

In a feat of physical prowess that impressed even him, he managed to get all the way to the third step from the bottom before he tripped over the hem. He slid to the bottom from there, cursing all the while.

"Where is the goddamned fire?" he growled as he flung the door open. And found himself staring into the eyes of an older woman he had definitely never met before. And she was soaking wet, even though it wasn't raining.

"Hello? Can I help you with something?" His voice was rough with sleep.

"You… are not Daphne."

"No, I'm her roommate. She's out of town. Are you okay?"

"Oh! Nice to meet you finally! I'm your landlord, Tabitha Spencer. I also live next door?"

He remembered now that their landlord lived in the other half of the house. Daphne had said she was traveling. But whatever, he could roll with it. That wasn't the most pressing concern.

"Nice to meet you. Are you okay, though? You're soaked through."

She looked down at herself, as if she'd forgotten. "Right. I need your help. I was going to ask Daphne but I guess you'll have to do. I woke up to find a pipe had burst, but I can't climb down into the basement with my knees the way they are. Can you help me?"

"Oh shit, of course." He slid his feet into his shoes and walked outside, glad it was only a few steps to the other brightly colored door. The chilly morning air on his bare chest left him shivering as he entered Mrs. Spencer's half of the house. It was laid out in a similar way to Daphne's, except when she led him to the open door next to her kitchen, water was running down the stairs in much larger quantities than he'd expected.

He could instantly see why she couldn't manage the stairs on her own—they were steep, poorly lit and covered in what he *hoped* were cobwebs.

But he wasn't letting himself think about spiders. She had come to him to ask for help. He wasn't going to chicken out over a mere possibility.

He steeled himself. "Where do I go to find the shutoff valve? I'll try to be fast."

"Down the stairs, all the way in the far back corner.

You'll probably have to climb over some boxes and crates, I'm afraid. It's pretty stuffed down there, as I recall. When you find it, just turn it clockwise and the water will turn off."

Turn it clockwise. He could handle that. He hoped.

Cade's phone rang just as he finished loading the last of the towels into the dryer. He'd known there would be tons of water to clean up, but he hadn't realized it would take every single towel in the entire duplex and then some.

Daphne's face smiled up at him from the phone screen, and he had to smile back as he answered. "When did you have time to put a selfie into my phone?"

"The other night at dinner when you went to the bathroom. Do you like it?"

He had to admit he did, and the laugh he got in return warmed him to his bones. "How was your brunch?"

"Oh, wonderful. Rook always had the best taste in friends, in my entirely biased opinion. I also learned they're both still looking for jobs for when they move back to Clover Hill next month. I thought it might solve a problem for the clinic, since Lily does medical billing and she's very personable."

Cade blinked. Was this how people got jobs in small towns? They just knew someone who happened to fit the requirements? "That would be convenient if he could afford her. I know Bryan's been having trouble finding someone qualified for his budget."

"I know. I figured it was worth a conversation, though. What's been happening with you? You hadn't replied to my texts this morning."

"Oh, I'm sorry. I've actually spent it with Mrs. Spencer."

"Our landlord? I didn't even know she was back in the country! Is there a problem?"

"Not on our end, mostly," he tried to reassure her. "She had a pipe burst this morning and couldn't get to the shutoff valve in the basement. We just finished cleaning up most of the water, so she's calling plumbers to see how fast they can get it fixed."

Judging from the cursing he heard from her kitchen, it wasn't going well.

"That turns the water off for our side of the house, too, doesn't it?"

"Yep. She says if she can't get it fixed today, she'll book us a room at the Bluestem until it is. Here's hoping it won't be necessary."

Daphne told him where the carrier was, just in case, then wrapped up the call with a promise from Cade to keep her updated.

The rehearsal went as smooth as butter. Daphne liked to think it had a large part to do with her masterful conducting, but realistically, it was more like the couple had chosen a very simple, heartfelt ceremony.

Still, when she sat down to the dinner she'd been invited to join, she felt a bone-deep relief that her job was finished for the night. She had seated herself with Kav and Bryan and a few of their former classmates and plus-ones, and everyone was having a great time catching up.

Just before the first plate was served, though, two familiar forms slid into the empty chairs opposite Daphne.

She looked up and froze with her wine glass halfway to her mouth. The woman sitting across from her was none other than her ex-girlfriend, Isobel Merino. And she was here with Rhys, who Daphne had grown up with.

Isobel looked good. Her cropped black hair curled ever so slightly over her forehead, showing off her perfect golden skin, immaculate makeup and a lush mouth that always seemed to be smiling.

It wasn't now, though. It was hanging open, as if she hadn't realized Daphne would be there, either.

They said each other's names at the same time. Daphne's voice sounded strangled. Isobel's was a quiet gasp.

"Oh, I didn't know you two knew each other," Rhys said.

Daphne closed her eyes and counted to ten before she spoke. "We, uh, used to date. I didn't know *you two* knew each other."

Rhys took a sip of his own drink. "What a small world. Isobel and I started dating a few months ago."

Isobel's mouth opened and closed like a fish as she looked between Daphne and Rhys, at a loss for words for the first time in Daphne's memory. She took pity on her ex.

"Ah, well, Rook hired me to plan the wedding. You know I could never turn xem down, especially given my experience."

"None of us ever could." The whole table, except for Isobel, laughed.

Rhys looked at his date, seemed to realize she was struggling to figure out where to look, then looked over Daphne's shoulder. "Oh, I see Miles. Excuse us, I've been wanting to ask her about something."

They rose and he tugged her around the back of the table.

"Well, *that* was awkward," Kav deadpanned. "Are you okay?"

Daphne didn't know how to answer the question, so she just shrugged. She had been shocked to see Isobel, sure, but that was the biggest emotion in her chest. There was none of the hurt and heartbreak she had felt the last time she'd seen her.

Someone else at the table decided to fill the silence with a story about how they'd met Rook and Lily. Everyone focused on the story, taking the spotlight off Daphne until the food arrived. She had never been so grateful to see a plate of food in her life.

After the toasts and speeches were finished, Daphne excused herself to use the restroom. Her two glasses of wine had run through her faster than expected, and she wanted to check in with Cade to see how Sushi was doing.

Daphne flushed and stepped out of the stall, only to squeak and step back at the unexpected appearance of the one person she hadn't really wanted to see.

"Oh my god, I can't seem to stop running into you tonight. I'm so sorry." Isobel said as she recognized her. Daphne stepped around her to the sink and began to wash her hands while the other woman continued to apologize.

"If I'd known you would be here I definitely wouldn't have come. I can find another restroom now. I'm so sorry."

She turned to go, but Daphne called out to her. "Izzy, it's okay." The nickname slid off her tongue just like old times, and it stopped Isobel in her tracks. "You can use the bathroom. You don't have to apologize. I'm not upset with you. Not anymore. Your parents... well, that's a different story."

That made Isobel laugh, then turn sober. "You and me both. It was so unfair of them to let you go. Your job should never have been a factor in our relationship, and I told them that. We fought about it pretty hard."

Somehow, that didn't surprise Daphne one bit. The elder Merinos were a united front against the world, but the heir to their empire had often opposed them when it came to the treatment of their employees and the future of the company.

"I appreciate it. I hope it makes a difference for future employees. Now, If you'll excuse me, I should get back out there."

"Wait!" A soft hand grabbed her upper arm, and Daphne halted. "I just wanted to say... you look good—happier—than you did before. And you've done a great job with the wedding. It's very right for the couple."

Daphne smiled genuinely at that. "Thank you. It means a lot, coming from you."

She could count on both hands the number of compliments Izzy had given her on her work in the years they'd known each other. Seeing it as the olive branch that it was, Daphne offered a compliment in return. "You look happier, too. I hope you and Rhys are good for each other. He's a great guy."

Isobel smiled back at her, a soft, shy smile that reminded Daphne of the way she had looked when they'd first started dating. "He is, thank you. Are you seeing anyone?"

"I am, actually. His name's Cade. It's pretty new."

"That's wonderful, Daphne. I hope you're happy together."

The sincerity of her words and a feeling of peace washed over her even as Isobel let that be her parting statement. Daphne hadn't expected to see Isobel again so soon, but she was glad she had.

It turned out the earliest a plumber could come to the house was Monday, so three hours later, Cade had bundled Sushi into her carrier and was standing in the Bluestem Bed and Breakfast's lobby.

It hadn't changed much in the few weeks since he'd last stayed there. The only difference was that the honey-suckle was blooming now and Helen Santos was wearing a sleeveless ocean blue jumpsuit that had a cape attached.

"You look *magical*," Cade told the woman. She beamed up at him.

"Why, thank you. Now, it's just the one room for you and our little feline friend? Not one for Daphne?"

He was surprised she was letting him stay with Sushi at all, but Tabitha had begged a favor from her old friend.

"Yes, ma'am. Just me and Sushi. Daphne's out of town until tomorrow. Hopefully we'll have water by then."

"Of course. Well, if you don't, you are welcome to stay another night. I only have one other guest this weekend, so Daphne can have her own room, too."

He heard the words, "Oh, she wouldn't need her own room. We mostly sleep together," come out of his mouth before he could stop himself.

He was fairly certain his entire upper body was bright red, but Helen gasped and clapped her hands delightedly.

"We *thought* you two were together, but we weren't sure! Oh, this is wonderful! You make such a fine couple."

Daphne was going to kill him for telling the town know-it-all they were together, but there was no stopping it now.

"Th—thank you, ma'am," he stammered. "A—are there any rules for Sushi? I've got her food and her litter box and she's generally well behaved. She shouldn't cause any problems."

Sushi chose that moment to whine about being in her carrier. Helen held her hands in front of her mouth like she was hiding a grin, but her eyes turned serious. "Try and make sure she doesn't, hm? I'm rather attached to the furniture in these rooms, and cat scratches in antique wood are difficult to repair."

He promised to do his best, and to pay for any damages, and she handed over the details brochure and room key, the same as last time.

He made his way up the stairs with the cat carrier, ready to take a nap.

ten

. . .

Cade woke with his stomach growling. Had he eaten today? He couldn't remember. When he opened his eyes, the room around him was pitch black. He blinked. What time was it?

His phone screen read 4:19 am, but that couldn't be right. It had been barely 3:00 pm when he'd gotten Sushi out of her carrier and let her explore the space. He'd planned to go to dinner, but there was basically no chance now.

Something else felt wrong, but he wasn't quite sure what. Stretching, his feet hit the edge of the full size bed and his arms the other. That was when he realized what it was.

Every time he had woken up since he'd moved to Clover Hill, he'd found Sushi sleeping either on top of him or next to him. And usually, she was purring or snoring.

But the bed was empty, and the room was too quiet. That was not a good sign.

"Sushi? Where are you, kitty?"

Nothing.

For the second time in as many days, he jumped out of bed in a hurry.

With a few quick motions, he had turned on all the lights in the room, hoping Sushi had just curled up somewhere else. But as he checked each nook and cranny, his worries grew. When he checked the windowsill above the radiator, he felt a chill on his skin that shouldn't have been there.

The window was open. He'd cracked it to get some air flow, but hadn't noticed there was no screen. Shit.

He let loose a slew of curses that probably woke whoever was in the room next to him, but he couldn't bring himself to care. He had to find this cat, and fast.

Several hours later, Cade was beginning to wonder if he would ever find the cat. He had knocked on all the neighbors' doors in both directions as soon as the sun had come out, asking them to keep an eye out for Sushi. They took his number and promised to call if they found her, but reassured him most cats knew how to find their way home.

Most cats might, but what if Sushi wasn't one of them? He kept catching himself crying, and he hoped the people who he'd talked to took pity on him.

He could only imagine what he looked like as he found himself in front of the first shop on the outskirts of downtown. He walked toward the front door of Reuben's, an ice cream and coffee shop, when a loud growl split the air.

There was only one kind of creature in the world that could make that kind of noise—cats fighting. It happened again, and this time, it echoed off something metallic.

They had to be near the dumpster to make that kind of noise.

He dashed around the building only to run straight into the open door of the shop so hard he fell backward into the dirt with a yelp.

"Shit, are you okay?" a bubbly feminine voice wondered from somewhere above him.

He looked up to find a short green-haired woman in a bright pink chef's coat closing the door in a hurry. Cade quickly cataloged his body and found himself to be well enough.

"Fine, I think," he said distractedly. "Did you see the cats?"

"That way!" She gestured to the alley. "I was trying to feed one but it kept running away. It sounds like it found a friend, though."

"Yeah, I think his friend is my roommate's cat," Cade grumbled. He started down the alley, but then turned around. He didn't know much about cats, but he knew when he was likely to be outmatched.

"Can I get your help, uh—I'm sorry. I don't know your name."

"Una! Una McGillicuddy," she said. "And I can absolutely help!"

Cade beamed at her. "Perfect. Do you have any boxes large enough to fit a cat in?"

Her face brightened. "I don't have any boxes, but I've got something that might work better. Give me a second."

She returned with two giant ice cream buckets. Cade grinned as he took his. Together, they stood side by side, blocking the alley with their bodies, and slowly advanced until they could see the cats.

Sure enough, there was Sushi, with her fur all puffed

out and hissing at the orange tabby across from her. She looked fierce, even with her floppy ears and complete lack of tail.

"Sushi, leave him alone and come here." He tried to keep his voice stern, but quiet. If he spooked them... he didn't want to think about that.

Sushi glanced at him, but didn't turn her face away from the threat. He started crooning to her in his most convincing tone, trying to get as close as he could without startling her. "Here, kitty. I'll keep you safe. I've got a nice, safe bucket for you..."

She let him approach, and when he was right behind her, he scooped the cat he knew into his bucket and slammed the lid down.

Una tried to grab the other. It yowled loudly, and all he saw was a puff of fur using her bright green head as a springboard to reach the top of the building. "Ow, ow ow ow!"

The tomcat disappeared onto the roof.

"Are you all right?"

The chef grinned at him. "I'm fine! I just hope the kitty didn't hurt himself jumping that far. My head's not a very good launching pad."

That made him laugh for the first time in hours. "Thank you so much! I'll, uh, bring this back later!"

Una nodded. Cade took off towards home at a sprint.

Tabitha had texted to say that the water would be back on by the time she got home, and Daphne was thrilled. She couldn't wait to get home to her own bed and to take a nice, hot bath. The wedding had turned out beautifully, but she was pretty sure she had never been this stressed out in her life.

When she pulled up in front of the house, all the lights were off and Cade wasn't answering his phone. She called him again and heard his ring tone coming from a different direction than she'd expected.

She turned toward the sound and startled.

Cade was barreling down the street toward them with a giant ice cream bucket in his arms. He was moving so fast, she was amazed a turbo flame didn't flow out behind him.

What in the hell?

He handed her the bucket and gestured for her to open it. She did and found her cat staring up at her. Her heart skipped a beat as she guessed what had happened.

"She got out, didn't she?"

Cade nodded, his hands on his knees, desperately trying to catch his breath.

"Knocked out... window screen... Spent... all day... looking. Found her... at Reuben's... fighting."

Shit. Reuben had mentioned that Una had been trying to catch a stray for a few weeks. Sushi must have found him. She had gotten both her rounds of shots, but what if the other cat had something nasty?

"Is she hurt? Do you know what happened?"

"Don't know.... Brought her home... so I could drive to the vet."

Right. She knew what to do. She had planned for an emergency like this.

"Take her and get in the car. I'll drive."

She drove as if there were no speed limit in Clover Hill, reaching the vet's office on the other side of town in a matter of minutes.

She jumped out of the car almost before it fully parked, running to the other side to get the bucket from Cade so he could get out.

A glance at the vet's office told her no one was there. She looked across the street and breathed a sigh of relief when Gina walked out of the mechanic's garage, confusion on her face.

"You two need help with something?"

And that was when Daphne burst into tears.

Gina let them into an exam room and checked Sushi in, flicking the lights on as she went, before she left them with some sage advice. "Go ahead and let her get settled while I get Dr. Tobiansky. I'm not sure what's going on, but I do know Sushi will be more comfortable out of that bucket."

Cade set the bucket on the exam table, holding it with one hand so it wouldn't roll. Daphne took the other gratefully when he held it out to her.

His hands were callused, but still soft, and he looked at her with red-rimmed, serious eyes. It broke Daphne's heart. Had he been crying over this?

"I'm so sorry. This should never have happened," he started, but she shook her head at him.

"It's not your fault. She's gotten out dozens of times and we've never had an issue. Murphy's Law says it had to happen sometime."

She knew her smile wavered, though, as Sushi crawled onto the table on her belly. She looked terrified. Daphne held out her other hand to the cat, who sniffed it, but stayed away. She wanted to say more, but the vet walked in.

Cade explained how Sushi had gotten into the bucket to the vet in slightly more detail than he'd given her previously, ending with, "and now we're here and I just really need her to be okay. Please, I'll pay whatever it takes."

Dr. Tobiansky gave him a soft smile. "Let me take a look and see what's going on. It's what I'm here for, after all."

The handhold turned from a comforting presence to Daphne clutching his hand in a death grip while the vet worked. Sushi meowed plaintively a few times, but otherwise didn't struggle.

Daphne couldn't help but hope that was a good sign. She didn't know what she'd do if Sushi was hurt.

"Well, it doesn't look like there's any obvious damage aside from a few scratches here by the scruff of her neck. There's no major lacerations and she isn't fighting me when I prod at places that would usually get injured in a cat fight. It looks like our little Sushi came out the victor in her battle. But you weren't able to get ahold of the other one?"

Cade shook his head. "Una tried, but he was pretty spry."

"I'll have to talk to her and see if we can't catch him," he said as he lowered Sushi. She yowled when her feet hit the table, then began to bathe herself.

The sound made Dr. Tobiansky frown. "Has she been doing that a lot? That kind of yell? And she's about six months old, right?"

Daphne shrugged. It hadn't happened a lot, but it wasn't uncommon. The Scottish Fold had always been a chatty cat.

"That combined with the constant attempts to escape might mean she's in heat. With her being out for a while, there's a good chance she might have gotten pregnant while she was out. There's no good way to tell for a couple of weeks, but I'll get you a pamphlet that talks about what to watch for."

"Is there anything we can do before then? Like… kitty Plan B?" She felt absurd asking for it.

Dr. Tobiansky shook her head. "We have medicine, but I don't want to use it unless we have to. It can have some nasty side effects. If you don't want kittens, the best way to fix it is to, well, fix *her*. I know that was planned for later this year, though."

Cade patted her hand sympathetically.

Daphne cursed herself, and her finances, and her cat's damn escape habits. Most of her money in the last year had gone toward the business. She had planned to have Sushi spayed after the next wedding was done, when she would have the funds to pay for it and time to be home with her to recover from the surgery.

She thanked the doctor for her help, and promised to keep an eye on Sushi. Cade thanked her too, brandishing his credit card, but she waved him off.

"No need for that. There's no charge for this. I'm always happy to alleviate concerns for my friends—furry and human."

Daphne smiled back at the vet, who was preparing to flick the lights out behind them.

"You are brilliant. If there's ever anything I can do for you, it's yours."

"I may take you up on that," she said with a laugh. "Now come on, let's get you all home. Sushi will be way happier in her own space than she would be here."

They grabbed Cade's and Sushi's things from the Bluestem on the way home. When they trudged into the house a few minutes later, they released the cat from her ice cream prison. She scampered under the couch. Cade couldn't blame her. She'd had a hell of a day, even if it had all been her own doing.

He stayed in the entryway holding the bucket. He just wanted to make sure Daphne was okay. If he had trusted someone with his pets and this had happened, he'd have freaked the hell out. But she hadn't yet.

After a few seconds, she turned to look at him and... smiled? Glancing down at himself, he realized just how much of a mess he looked. He was wearing his usual workout attire, but that was all that was normal about him. He could feel his hair sticking out at all angles, like he'd been running his hands through it all day. When he'd toed off his shoes in the entry, it had revealed he was wearing mismatched socks—something she had never seen him do before.

"You look like you could use a hug."

"God, you have no idea," he breathed, stepping into her arms. When he wrapped his arms around her in return, he couldn't help thinking, no matter what happened, everything would be okay as long as they could just hold each other at the end of the day.

Cade didn't know how long they stood there just holding each other. Neither of them said anything, just took comfort in their new partner's presence.

It was long enough, though, that the kitty cause of all his problems felt safe enough to poke her head out from under the sofa and meow at them.

At the sound, Daphne slid her arms from around his

waist with a crooked smile. "Our master has forgiven us, it seems."

Cade snorted, thinking it was more likely Sushi had realized it was dinner time, but he released Daphne. When she stepped away, it felt like he had lost a limb.

He went and got a can of wet food and just emptied it into the cat's bowl. Hopefully that would earn him back some goodwill. The cat glared at them suspiciously, but she ate heartily. That was good, especially if the tomcat in the alley had actually gotten it in.

"Do you know what you'll do if she is pregnant?"

"Well, I guess we'll have kittens," Daphne sighed. "Getting her fixed is expensive and not something I'll have the money for until well after the kittens would be born. That's why I'd waited in the first place."

It made sense, from the conversation in the vet's office. He also knew he could help. "You know I can help pay to fix her. I'm more than willing. After all, this is a little my fault."

Daphne shook her head. "It's really not, Cade. Sushi is my responsibility. The vet told me this was gonna happen if I didn't get her fixed, and here we are. It's not ideal, but I think I can adopt out any kittens she has. She's awfully cute."

He had to admit that was true, even as annoyed with the cat as he was. If her kittens turned out anything like their mother, people would be tripping over themselves to bring one home. And if she was sure, he had to respect that. But it didn't mean he had to leave her to handle it all on her own when it was his fault this had happened in the first place.

"Then, if the kittens come, I'll help you take care of them and pay for their first round of shots," he promised.

"I appreciate it, Cade, so much. If it comes down to it, I may just take you up on that."

Daphne stretched her arms over her head, turning side to side in a movement that made a series of cracks and pops that concerned him.

"Does your back hurt? I can help with that, at least."

She smiled at him. "I've got giant boobs, Cade. My back always hurts. Plus, I spent almost the entire weekend on my feet. I'll be okay, though."

He waggled his eyebrows at her. "Are you sure? I've got some massage skills I'd be happy to practice on you."

Her smile spread into a wicked grin. "I am never going to turn a massage down. Lead the way, Giant Man."

eleven

· · ·

Daphne arrived at Cracked Up Chiropractic just after one o'clock on Monday afternoon. The building had changed dramatically since she had last seen it, but she had to say she was impressed.

The soft ivory, dark brown, and forest green palette worked well on the small building, pulling the same colors from the furniture through the window. She had to give herself a little pat on the back for picking it, but then she saw the logo painted on the newly uncovered window. That logo, which used the business's name to look like a person's shoulders and spine, was all Bryan. All together, it was kind of perfect.

The front door was locked. She jiggled the handle and peered in, hoping one of the men would see her, but it didn't look like anybody was there. She knocked harder and was rewarded. Cade stepped out of one of the back rooms, shading his eyes against the bright afternoon light.

His face melted into a smile that warmed her even more than the June sun on her back. He crossed the room in three long strides and unlocked the door. She stepped in and relished the cool air.

"Hey, you. Did I know you were coming to visit?" He pressed a kiss to her lips that was over way too soon. "Not that I'm not happy to see you! But Bryan said our social media guru was on their way, so…"

She struck a pose. "And she is at your service!"

His eyes widened. "You're a social media guru in addition to being a wedding planner?"

She laughed. "Well, they kind of go hand in hand. Most people find their wedding planners on social media, so I've had to get good at it."

"And we are all very lucky," Bryan called from his office. "Come on back, you two. I'm gonna grab lunch for everybody from Wong's. What do you two want?"

They called in their orders for pickup, then watched the lanky man cross the street, leaving them alone. Cade gave her a brief tour of the changes they had made and she was surprised at how comfortable it felt. She still knew she was in a chiropractor's office—the spine health posters and equipment wouldn't let you forget it—but it didn't feel clinical.

"You guys have done a great job getting this place set up. I honestly didn't expect Bryan to be able to pull this together so fast, or that it would look this good."

Cade stuck his hands in his pockets and shrugged. "Honestly, I've mostly been manual labor and tech support. Most of this was his vision."

Daphne was absolutely sure he was downplaying his part in this, and she wasn't going to let him get away with it. "Not to hear him tell it. At the wedding, he wouldn't shut up about how many great ideas you've had and how you wanted him to get hanging plants since there's so much natural light with the windows uncovered." Her expression turned teasing, "If I hadn't known where both your and his affections lay, I would've wondered if something untoward was happening here."

He laughed and waved her off, but Daphne saw the blush on his cheeks. "He would've gotten there without me. I just helped him get there faster. I will never be sorry that I came out here, though I will regret it if he doesn't let me get some hanging plants. Can't you imagine a couple of hoyas in the windows and a snake plant or two in some of the dead spaces?"

"I... I could if I knew what those were? I don't actually know much about plants."

"Oh, let me show you! I've got some at home." He whipped out his phone and scrolled through his pictures with a speed that surprised her. Then he showed her a picture of a hanging plant that seemed to be all leaves. "This is a hoya carnosa, and I think they'd be great for the windows. And then... this is a snake plant."

When she exclaimed she had seen those before, Cade rumbled his deep laugh. "That doesn't surprise me. Snake plants are everywhere in offices and things. If I knew a place I could get some locally, I think they'd be perfect here. Did you know they're actually pretty good at filtering air? And they don't have flowers, so they're basically allergen-free unless someone eats them."

He kept talking, telling her all sorts of things about the snake plant. She didn't think she had seen him get so excited about anything in the time she had known him and she adored it. She had no idea what most of what he was saying meant, but she loved listening to the sound of his voice.

"You know, if those are as common as you say, we

might be able to get some from Four Leaf. Lawrence has gotten better about stocking basic stuff in the last year or so, he might have something workable."

Cade's eyes went so wide Daphne thought they would literally sparkle with excitement if they were in an animated television show. "Clover Hill has a *plant store*? I could have had plants all this time? How am I just now learning this?"

"I'm surprised you didn't know! It's right down the street, next to Reuben's. I know you've been there."

He snorted. "Only because your cat decided she needed to get lucky. Oh, that reminds me, I should see if he wants his ice cream bucket back. I can't imagine it can be reused, but it's the polite thing to do, right?"

"Right." Daphne agreed. "Tell you what, how about we swing by Four Leaf and Reuben's once I'm done teaching your technophobe boss how to use the internet? I'm sure he can spare you for a business adventure."

A rush of warm air hit her back and she sighed. "He's right behind me, isn't he?"

Cade nodded, trying and failing to suppress a smile.

"This *technophobe* just bought your lunch, so be nice to me. And yes, you can go plant shopping once you've taught me how to use Tic Tac or whatever it is."

Bryan held out a bag of food to each of them. Daphne heaved a dramatic sigh, but took the offered bag from her friend. At least she'd have a full belly for what was sure to be a long afternoon.

Cade practically bounced down the street, he was so excited. He had no idea how he'd missed a plant store in

Clover Hill, but he couldn't wait to see what fun things they would have. Even better, he got to do it with Daphne by his side. She kept looking up at him and smiling, and it made him feel like the most important man in the world.

Daphne pulled him to a stop in front of quite possibly the smallest store he'd ever seen. Out front on one side, there were some false sunflowers and other plants that looked native on a shelf with a QR code underneath text about making good planting choices. On the other side was a shelf full of cactuses, succulents and terrarium building supplies. Every square foot of the interior of the space was filled with plant shelves with the teensiest possible walkway down the center. It looked like heaven.

"Welcome to Four Leaf Plants!" a cheerful man called from the small walkway. He was much thinner than Cade, but was tall enough to be able to meet his gaze easily with a grin as wide as his face. Cade liked him instantly.

"Oh, hi, Daphne. Are you here to buy more cacti to kill? Or is your new friend better with plants than you are?"

Daphne was blushing when Cade turned to look at her. "No, I'm not here for me. I've given up the plant life. Lawrence tried his hardest to help me keep things alive, but, well, you've seen my schedule," she explained. That didn't surprise him. Cactuses were remarkably finicky if you didn't know what you were doing.

"Actually, my partner here loves plants, and he wants some for Cracked Up Chiropractic."

"Ah, you must be Cade. The whole town's been talking about you these last few weeks. It's a pleasure to meet you." The man—Lawrence—held out his hand and Cade shook it firmly. "Did you have anything in particular in mind, or would you like some guidance?"

Cade explained what he was looking for, and why. Lawrence's grin sparkled in the sunlight.

"I have just the plants for you, my boy. Stay right there."

He turned, grabbed the shelf of plants and, to Cade's surprise, pulled it out onto the sidewalk where they stood. Once it had reached the open air, it folded open to reveal even more plants—including the ones he needed. He had never seen anything like it, but he loved it.

"That is an amazing contraption! How do you make sure your plants get the right amount of sunlight?"

"Isn't it excellent? When no one's in the shop, I keep it open and rotate it regularly."

Clearly it was working. Every plant on the shelf looked as healthy as could be, and several were even flowering. He saw one he thought he recognized in the back, and an idea occurred to him.

"Oh, that's so smart. Daphne, have you seen this? Isn't it the coolest thing?"

She was standing a little further away from him than he remembered, with an expression on her face like she was watching something adorable.

"Yes, sweetie, it's very cool. Does he have what you need, though?"

"Oh! Yes!" He reached forward and grabbed two of the trailing pothos plants, showing her their heart-shaped leaves. "Wouldn't these be perfect in the windows? Once they grow some more, we can drape them across the beam and make them into a living wall hanging."

He set those on the ground beside him and then grabbed two buckets of tall plants that were all leaves. "These are snake plants. They're really low maintenance except for needing a pretty wide pot. I bet we can get those here, right, Lawrence?"

Lawrence laughed. "Of course. I've got some planters from the artist commune that might suit you. Let me get them from the back."

He returned with a rolling cart containing several beautifully colored clay pots—one was a charcoal gray that faded to white, one had a bright pink and blue stripe, and the third was a swirl of purple and yellow.

This, he was leaving up to Daphne. "Which one do you think would look best in the clinic?"

"You need two, right? For the two plants?" At Cade's nod, she studied them carefully. "I think the charcoal and white for the front desk and the swirly one for the back corner by the x-ray room. It could use some life in it. What do you think?"

Cade beamed at her, thrilled with her choices. "I think that will be perfect! Though… I am thinking maybe we should have brought the car. This is a little much for even me to carry in one trip. Would you be willing to walk back and get my rental?"

She wrinkled her nose at him. "You do love making a girl walk everywhere. Yes, I will. You've got Bryan's card, right?"

At Cade's nod, she began to walk back down the street. He turned back to the proprietor with said card in hand. "I'd like to buy all of these, please, including the pots."

"We can take care of that. Can I offer you some appropriate potting mix for these beauties?"

"Oh, yeah, that would be smart. Enough for all the pots, please."

He rang up the total, a number Cade knew was more than fair.

"Now that she's gone… is that a bromeliad I see in the corner?"

Lawrence raised his eyebrows but nodded.

"I don't think even Daphne could kill one of those, and they're safe for pets. Can I get one of those and one of your largest terrarium logs? I want to pick them up tomorrow morning so I can surprise her with it."

The words brought the smile back to the older man's face. "Oh, now that's a nice gesture. You sure can. The ladies love a surprise every once in a while. It keeps the relationship fresh!"

"Yes, sir," he laughed. "I'll keep that in mind. Thank you for all your help. If you'd like to come see us for our soft opening on the 15th, we'd be happy to show you what we're about."

Lawrence nodded. "I'll try and swing by. Helen's been bothering me to get my back checked out for years. Maybe now's a good time."

Cade hoped he would.

Daphne spent the next day wrapped up with Amber and Hari's impending nuptials. She was spending a little more time with them in person than some of her other couples, but she didn't mind. They were more than a decade younger than her, but she liked them.

Today had been the final walk-through of Juniper Breeze Park with Laura, the city manager. The beautiful butch lesbian stood as the de facto head of the park, so she had to approve all their temporary structures. She also had some advice about where to place the tents and things for the best view for the guests, and where good places to take photos would be. The young women had been effusive with their thanks as they punched their notes into their phones.

As much as she liked them, though, she was excited to get home. Cade had promised to cook her a nice dinner, and she was looking forward to seeing what he would make. Everything he had made from his meal kits had looked tasty, but she wasn't sure if those were really his cooking style.

It would also be their first real date as a couple, and it made her feel a little bit giddy. They had found a lovely rhythm at home, despite their backward start to the relationship. They got ready together each morning, taking turns cooking breakfast and doing the dishes, and then went off to do their jobs. After work, she would help him do the prep work for the meal kit—he cooked and she cleaned up. They made a good team, since her culinary knowledge only consisted of the various breakfast foods she'd learned to cook in college.

Tonight, though, would be special. She could feel it, even as she drove home from the park. When she pulled up to the house, her giant man stood on the front porch wearing a ruffled apron she had never seen before and the dimpled grin she loved so much.

Daphne whipped her phone out of the console and took a picture. She wanted to remember this night.

The house smelled absolutely divine when he led her into it, but she couldn't tell what it was. When she asked him, he said he'd just have to show her. He had a surprise for her first.

Instead of leading her to the dining room, he took her to a corner of the living room that had once held a sculpture Kav liked. Now, it held an end table with a tall, brightly colored plant in a simple black and white pot she recognized immediately.

"You bought me a plant when you sent me to get the car?" The words came out more accusatory than she had intended. She softened her tone. "It's beautiful."

"This is a bromeliad. It's cat safe, even if she eats it, and it's very easy to take care of. Basically, all you have to do is make sure it gets some indirect sunlight and keep the cup part of the flower full of water. There's no fussing with the soil at all."

She heard everything he was saying, but as she stared at the beautiful plant, all she could feel was the impending failure.

"Cade, what if I kill it? You heard Lawrence. I'm terrible with plants. I can't even keep cactuses alive. I basically have a black thumb!" Her anxiety leaked into her voice before she could stop it.

He grabbed both of her hands in his and forced her to look him in the eye. "I understand you think you can't care for plants, but I believe in you. You can do anything you want to do, no matter how hard it is. You prove it every day, in everything you do. And you can do this."

The earnestness in his words and on his face made her burst into tears. No one but Kav had ever said they believed in her to do something she was scared of. And plants scared her, for whatever reason. She knew it was silly to be crying over the potential future death of a plant, but there she was.

"How can you already believe in me so much?

"Because I've never seen you faced with a problem that was bigger than you could handle. You and a binder can tackle anything you set your mind to. And, you aren't alone in this. I love plants, and I love you and I can help you."

She looked up at him, a little shocked. "You love me?"

His jaw dropped as he realized what he'd said. "Um, I —I wasn't planning on telling you yet but I guess the cat's out of the bag. I'm falling in love with you, Daphne."

That made her laugh. "I'm falling in love with you, too, Cade. And I meant to say that."

He laughed softly and pulled her into an embrace. Like always, it made everything feel right. He smelled of sweat and sage and... croissants? That was a new smell for him.

She pulled back from him to eye him suspiciously. "Why do you smell like croissants?"

He let her go, laughing so hard tears welled up in his eyes, too. "Because I made beef Wellington. I got puff pastry from Flakey Bakey Hearts, but I made everything else myself. Come on. It should be cool enough to slice now."

Daphne thought she had never felt quite so taken care of. She could get used to this.

twelve

. . .

"Now, you come back and see us anytime. And tell your friends about us!" Bryan called after the last customer.

It was a woman Cade recognized from Flakey Bakey Hearts but whose name he couldn't remember for the life of him. He'd had a lot of moments like that over the course of the soft opening. It didn't matter, though. If they came back to be a patient, he would learn their names then.

When everyone had finally left, Bryan locked the door and then leaned against it as if he needed the support. Cade understood completely.

"We did it, folks. We made it through our first day," Bryan announced with a grin.

The new secretary, Lily, let out a loud whoop. Cade understood the feeling, though he was a little too tired for theatrics of his own. They had put in a hard day's work.

He hadn't thought the town was that big, but there had been a steady stream of people wanting to learn more about what they were doing and what their price range was. He felt like he had been in customer service mode all day, with very few breaks aside from lunch and calls to

Doc to answer some questions his replacement had had. He was exhausted.

Lily had done pretty well, and Cade could see why Daphne liked her so much. She had had a few questions about the Chirotouch software when she was booking new patients, but Bryan had been able to help her through it. Her spouse, Rook, had come by for lunch and they'd all had a great time. He was glad. They would need to be able to rely on each other once Cade's time there was up.

And under their agreement, there was exactly one month left. That was the other reason. He hadn't wanted to ask until the business was actually open, but he couldn't stop thinking about how much he wanted to stay in Clover Hill. Especially as the people he had gotten to know from the grocery store and various outings with Daphne showed up in full force for Bryan and Kav. Even the ones who didn't know them well.

He wanted to stay with Daphne, wanted to see what was possible for their future. It was still early days and he wanted more time. He thought, hoped, Daphne did too. But it wasn't completely under their control. He had to talk to Bryan about his future at Cracked Up Chiropractic, and he couldn't put it off any longer.

They each wiped down their spaces, then Bryan went back to his office while Cade gathered the trash. Lily left them behind with a cheerful "See you tomorrow!" that made him smile. When everything was where it belonged, he made his way back to the office and groaned.

Bryan was listening to Billy Joel, and dancing almost exactly the same way his father did at work parties.

"God, you are your father's son," he laughed, though he wasn't sure if he was horrified or amused.

Bryan whirled around with a hand to his chest, clearly

startled by Cade's voice. Then his cheeks and ears flushed red as he realized he had been caught dancing.

"I thought you'd left already!"

"What, you think I'd leave without congratulating you on a good opening day? You know better by now."

"I do know better," Bryan sighed, sinking down into his office chair and pausing the music. "Today really did go well, didn't it?"

"I've been part of three other openings and... yeah, it went really well," he assured the other man. "Lily got at least seven people signed up for an introductory session that I saw, and I heard a couple people say they needed to check their calendars before they scheduled anything. That's a really good day."

Bryan's presence became sunnier with every word Cade said, to his relief. "I *thought* so, but it's so hard to tell what's a good visitor-to-patient ratio, you know?"

Cade did know. And, lucky for Bryan, he knew, "We're going to get a lot of lookie-loos for the next week or so, but between starting to see patients and our planned outreach events, you should see the number of appointments grow. If things are light for a little while, though, it's okay. You can always reduce the number of days you're in the office to help cut down on costs if you need to. But I don't think you'll need to."

"You are a blessing, you know that? I don't know how I would've done this without you."

The words warmed Cade to the bone. It was always nice to feel appreciated, especially when you were about to beg for a job you weren't sure was even available. He knew he wasn't going to get a better segue than that.

"So... since we're open for real, I wanted to talk to you about my role here."

Bryan's thick eyebrows drew down. "What do you mean? You're not trying to leave me early, are you? I mean, I'll understand if—"

"No, no, let me finish," Cade interrupted. "I wanted to tell you...to ask you..." For as much as he'd thought about this, he would have thought it'd be easier to get the words out. He was surprised Bryan didn't interrupt him back when he took a deep breath. "I want to stay in Clover Hill. I wanted to talk to you about whether there was a chance for me to stay on here at Cracked Up Chiropractic after the grand opening. I know you've been looking at other physical therapists already, but... I wanted to put my name in the ring."

There. It was out. And Bryan wasn't staring at Cade as if he had three heads. That had to be a good sign. He was, however, blinking owlishly while he thought.

"You... don't want to go back to Pop's place? I thought you liked being there."

"I did. I do. I love working for your father. But... he's got someone else doing my job now and... well, things have changed for me and Daphne—" He froze, realizing she might not have told him yet. He hadn't said anything about their relationship, either. Bryan smiled at him.

"My partner told me about you and Daphne, not that they had to. It was obvious you two had a connection, and when Kav mentioned something was going on there... I didn't say anything, because it's none of my business what my employees do in their free time. I hope that's not weird."

"Not weird," Cade laughed. "It actually makes this a little easier." He should have known his boss could tell. Even if he hadn't known Cade that well at first, Bryan had dated Daphne's best friend for years. He had to know her, too.

"Right. So, I'm gonna be frank with you, Cade. I would love to keep you here. I want to keep Daphne happy, and you seem to be doing a great job of that. I also think you're great at this and would make a great manager here. But…" He let out his breath in a gust and dropped his gaze to the desk with a frown. "I don't think the business can afford to pay you what you're worth. You've been in this business for a long time, and you're a manager at Pop's place. I can't match that. My savings wouldn't have even covered your salary the last few months, and even if things pick up as quickly as you think… things are going to be very tight for a while. I've been applying for grants wherever I can, but… I don't want to get your hopes up and not have them pan out."

That was a kindly worded *no* if Cade had ever heard one. Cade ran his fingers through his hair to try and hide his disappointment. He felt as if someone had dumped a bucket of ice water over his head. The worst part was, he understood what Bryan was saying. He knew there wasn't much in the way of a budget, and that any child of Doc's would be horrified at the idea of paying someone less than they were worth.

"I appreciate the honesty, Bryan. I completely understand if you can't hire me, but I wanted to talk to you before I started figuring out my next steps."

"I will see if there is anything I can do for you, Cade. I promise that."

He tried to smile, but he felt like it got mangled on its way to his face. "Thanks, boss. And, uh, I'd appreciate this if you didn't mention it to Doc. I haven't talked to him yet."

"Of course. That's a conversation you two need to have with each other. But, I know he would want to help you if he can. Don't wait too long to talk to him."

Cade knew Bryan was right. Doc was just that kind of person. "Thanks, Bryan. I'll get out of your hair now."

Bryan's smile was a lot sadder than it had been before this conversation. "I'll see you tomorrow, Cade."

Cade's smile became a little more real as he gathered his things and walked out the door, headed home to the woman he didn't think he was going to be able to stay with.

It was official. Daphne was going to be a grandparent. They'd visited the vet and Dr. Tobiansky had confirmed it. By the end of July, she and Cade would have an unknown number of even tinier furry bodies to tend to.

At least she wouldn't be alone in taking care of them. She didn't know how much assistance newborn kittens would need, but she was definitely going to be taking Cade up on his promise to help as much as he could before he had to leave. She'd even picked up a greeting card from a local seller that read "It's a baby!" to break the news to him. Hopefully, he'd find the crossed out word *baby* and a *kitten* scribbled in as funny as she did. He could use the cheering up.

He'd seemed down ever since the soft opening, but whenever Daphne asked about it, he'd smiled and said he just had a lot on his mind. She knew she couldn't force him to talk about it, but hoped he would share eventually..

She'd just gotten home with their dinner—carryout from Weathervane—when Cade got home. She greeted him with a cheerful welcome, only for her smile to fade as she took in his stiff posture and downcast expression. "What's wrong?"

He shuffled his feet and looked at the floor while he answered her. "Bryan hired a full-time physical therapist today." He slumped now, looking entirely defeated, and her heart broke, even though she wasn't sure *why* this was bad news.

"This is good news, isn't it? Why don't you seem more excited?"

He wouldn't meet her gaze, but he answered her in an even voice. "Well, I had been hoping that... maybe he would want to hire me and I could stay here. If... if that's something you would want."

The card she'd had in her hands fluttered to the counter. She'd had no idea it was even under consideration, but now that it was out there... she wanted it more than anything.

"Oh, honey!" She crossed the room in a few steps and wrapped him in her arms. "This is what you've been worried about all week, isn't it? Why didn't you say anything?"

He nodded into her hair. "I didn't know how to talk to you about it. I just don't want this to be over before we've even had a chance to really try."

"I don't either," she whispered. "But...if you really want to stay... I might be able to help?"

For the first time that night, he met her gaze. She could see the heartache and confusion in his hazel eyes. "What do you mean? Bryan basically told me there was no chance he could hire me, and there's only three weeks before my contract is up."

That made her smile. "Do you remember what you said when we first got together?"

He scratched his chin. "Uh... vaguely? Something along the lines of 'we could have some fun first and figure out the rest later?'"

Daphne smiled. "Basically. You also said I was very smart, and you were very flexible, and between the two of us, we could figure out a solution."

That got a soft chuckle out of him. "Sounds like me."

"Well, if you are open to some help, I think I know what we can do. Will you trust me?"

"I have no idea what you're about to suggest, but I absolutely trust you."

Daphne pulled her arms from around his waist and he let her go on instinct. Faster than he'd ever seen her move before, she dashed up the stairs. She came back down a few seconds later at the same speed, almost tripping over Sushi where she napped on the floor. She skidded to a halt in front of him and, with eyes and grin sparkling, presented a green three-ring binder like it was the answer to all of their problems.

He blinked at it, trying to figure out what he was missing without asking. But he was too tired to use that much brainpower. "I think I need an explanation."

That made her laugh. He didn't think he would ever get tired of hearing it, even if it was sort of directed at him at the moment.

"I think best when everything is on paper in front of me," Daphne explained. "I've got one of these for every event I've ever done on my own from the initial pitch to how everything ended up going. I've also done them for every time Kav and I have gone job hunting, and it has never failed us. If, well…" Her smile turned a bit pensive. "You're sure you want to stay? You've mentioned that you loved working for Dr. Schwartz. You could always go home again and we could try long distance, if you wanted."

He shook his head. He didn't want that. "We've got something really great going on here, and I love working with Doc, it's true. But… I love it here with you more."

Her expression brightened and she squeezed his hand. "Well, if Bryan can't find the money for you, we're going to have to find someone who can."

He wasn't sure what would go in a binder for a job hunt. Wasn't all of that digital nowadays? But it had been a long time since he'd had to job hunt, so he would take all the help he could get. She had asked him to trust her, and he'd said yes. So he was going to trust her.

He took a deep breath and took the binder from her. "Where do we start?"

She beamed at him. "With dinner. There's no sense in letting it get any colder. Afterwards, we update your résumé and start hunting for jobs."

Suddenly, the scent of enchiladas filled his nose, and he whirled to find the bag from Weathervane on the table.

"Has food been there the whole time I've been home?" he asked incredulously. He had never in his life failed to notice there was food in the room. He'd known he was preoccupied, but this was next level.

Daphne laughed again, leading him. "I haven't learned how to teleport food yet, so, yes. Don't worry, I won't tell Yesenia. Imagine how offended she would be!"

Having met the chef twice now, Cade had no trouble imagining the outraged expression on her face. He had no interest in offending the wonderful woman who made the best side salad he had ever tasted.

Daphne handed him one of the salads and he opened it. It smelled amazing and had at least two dozen different types of plant matter in there.

Maybe, if he was really lucky, Yesenia would someday tell him some of the ingredients so he could recreate it at home. For now though, he drizzled the raspberry balsamic vinaigrette over the top and dug in. Daphne had, too.

"That reminds me, she wanted me to ask you and Bryan if there was any chance you would be willing to open earlier one morning in a week so she could come and see you without having to find someone to cover her duties in the kitchen. She's been having some leg pain she'd like to get checked out."

"That's not a bad idea," he said between bites. "I'm sure there's plenty of other folks working night shift or who commute that would be glad to take an early morning slot."

He punched a reminder into his phone to talk to Bryan about it tomorrow. He was sure his boss would love this new way to accommodate the community. And he was glad to be able to help someone he liked so much.

With that done, he opened the steaming container of enchiladas and grabbed one of the pulled pork and goat cheese ones. He was going to need the energy to get his brain working.

Once they'd cleared the table, Daphne sent him upstairs for his laptop and the printer. When he got back, he found that she had opened her own laptop and shared the screen where she was job hunting on the television.

He made quick work of updating his résumé before emailing the file to Daphne and printing a copy for the binder.

"This looks good. It's no wonder Bryan can't afford to hire you. I mean, you've basically been doing this since you got your certificate at... nineteen?"

She looked impressed. He blushed. "For the most part. There were a few years where I was a part-time physical therapist and part-time teacher at a gym. That was pretty fun."

Daphne furrowed her brow and looked back at the screen, mouthing along with what she was reading. "When was that? I don't see it on here."

"Oh, that was when I was twenty-two when I was working at Symmetric. They paid well but the hours were really low. That's how I learned to teach the classes Bryan and I have been doing."

She tossed a pillow at him. "Put that on there! That's big experience you're not showing with the other jobs. Plus, it's what you want to do more of, right?"

She was right and he told her so. Then he did what she had advised, printing a new copy and sliding it into the first plastic sleeve.

Now that that was done, they went through the job listings together. Cade was surprised by how many places in a decent commuting range were looking for a physical therapist or wellness teacher. Every time they found one he was interested in, Daphne added the link to the email chain and printed the page with the details and requirements for the binder.

He finally understood why Daphne loved her binders so much. He would have to go back and actually write cover letters and apply for each of the jobs, but he had concrete evidence of everything he could do and had done. And for the first time in a week, he began to hope again.

thirteen

. . .

The first weekend of July found Daphne surrounded by sunflowers. Amber and Hari's florist had gone all out, just as they'd requested, and they were all thrilled with the results.

Of course, the real joy of the day was that the lovely young couple was finally, officially married. It seemed like the entire town had come out to celebrate with them in Juniper Breeze Park, and the women looked absolutely radiant.

Finally, when all the vendors were paid and cleanup was underway, Daphne could leave. Or, well, she could have if she had driven herself. Kav had been having car trouble, so Daphne had loaned them her beloved buggy. Cade had dropped her off earlier in the day, and now she stood at the entrance to the park looking at the stars while she waited.

A car pulled up beside her, but it wasn't Cade. She ignored it in favor of searching for the Big Dipper, sure they'd drive on. She loved the way that no matter how big Clover Hill got, you could always see the constellations.

She didn't think she ever wanted to live in a place where it wasn't possible.

Someone cleared their throat nearby, and she looked over to find Helen leaning out of the sedan. The older Greek woman had her eyebrows raised and a smile on her lips, as if it wasn't the first time she'd made a sound.

"Hi, Helen."

"You need a ride, dearie? Or are you just enjoying the scenery?"

"Oh, no thank you. Cade is on his way to get me."

Helen studied Daphne's face. She didn't know what Helen was looking for, but she apparently found it.

"I'll wait with you, if you don't mind. Let me just park."

Daphne didn't think she really had a choice, but she didn't mind.

"I'm surprised Lawrence isn't with you. I could've sworn he was on the RSVP List." Daphne wondered. She was also sure she'd seen them together on the dance floor at one point during a slow point. They had been together for years, but didn't want the world to know for whatever reason. Of course, this was Clover Hill, and they were not particularly subtle people.

"Oh, he went home hours ago. He enjoys the food and the company, but after a while he likes to go back to his plants. Me, I like to dance until the night is done." She shimmied a little for emphasis, her sparkly dress catching the light of the stars and the bus stop light. They laughed together, then fell into companionable silence.

"You know, you did a really good job with this wedding," Helen said out of the blue. "I've held my share of events at the Bluestem, as you know. It isn't as easy as it looks to have an event. People always know when you get something wrong. Amber and Hari were very nervous, but you had it all under control and everything moved really smoothly for us guests."

Daphne stared at the older woman. Helen had always been straightforward and willing to tell you where you could improve, no matter who you were. Unadulterated praise was almost unheard of.

"Thank you," she said sincerely. "That means a lot coming from you."

Helen patted her cheek with a soft hand. "I hope others told you the same. Many of us have noticed how well you've done on your own. In fact I have a proposition for you."

"Oh?"

"With all these new businesses and people in town, I am finding that the Bluestem events calendar is busier than I can handle on my own. I was wondering if, perhaps, you might be interested in a partnership with me. You'd be well compensated, of course."

Daphne gaped at the bed and breakfast owner. "Helen, are you serious?"

"Of course I'm serious, silly girl. You think I would make this kind of offer as a joke?"

Of course she didn't. But... she couldn't wrap her head around it. Their events were much smaller than the weddings she'd spent the summer on, mostly company retreats and events for some of the other local businesses, but they were consistent. That kind of steady business would mean she would be able to justify the expense of an actual office of her own, maybe even hire an assistant. It would be game-changing.

"I would love to sit down and talk with you about what exactly you're looking for. I don't want to promise something I can't deliver without seeing the details, but I would love to work with you and the Bluestem. When would be a good time for that?"

Helen checked her phone's calendar and offered up a date and time. Daphne agreed, punching it into her own. That was when Daphne remembered that if anyone would know about a new rental... "By the way, do you happen to know anyone renting out a small, cat-friendly apartment?"

Helen pursed her lips. "I will see what I can find out for you. Maybe something with a gym for that man of yours."

Cade pulled up before she could say anything else, not even a thanks.

"Hey, sweetheart. Hey, Ms. Helen. Do you need a ride home, too?"

The older woman just shook her head. "I can manage my own self just fine. Your girl did good work today. Take her home."

Cade smiled, his one dimple glowing with caught moonlight. "Yes, ma'am."

In the weeks since they'd started making real plans to stay together, Daphne had booked a few new weddings going into the fall and winter, and now they knew she'd have enough small work from the Bluestem to be able to stay in her current home without a roommate, which was a huge relief.

At least he didn't have to worry about whether she would have to move if he couldn't find work.

That last part was the real concern.

Cade was starting to feel like he had interviewed for

every physical therapist job in the state. He knew that was a little overdramatic, but having done more than a dozen interviews in two weeks was a lot. Even worse, he was only waiting on word from two of them. The others had immediately said he wasn't a good fit for the position for one reason or another.

It was soul sucking, but he couldn't give up. Each rejection had just strengthened his need to work harder to find something, anything, that would let him stay here. He'd even talked to Doc about it, having needed to use him as a reference. With every day, he was falling harder and faster in love with Daphne. He wasn't going to let capitalism get in the way of that love.

fourteen

. . .

With a flourish, the mayor cut the ribbon stretched across the clinic's doors with the largest, glitziest pair of scissors Daphne had ever seen.

"Cracked Up Chiropractic is officially open for business," they declared, and the crowd cheered—it felt like the whole town was there. "Now go have some fun!"

She took up her post next to the bouncy house, making sure to only let so many kids in at once and asking the rest to form an orderly line. One of the parents joked Bryan was providing it so the kids would need to come in and see him when they inevitably dinged themselves up, and everyone around them laughed. She supposed they were entitled to a little dark humor, given children's propensity for injuring themselves.

Her phone rang halfway through getting the second round of kids into the house. It was Tabitha. What could she be calling about? "Hello?"

"Daphne? This is Tabitha. Can you hear me?" It was hard to hear over the sound of the kids bouncing around next to her, so she walked a little further away and pressed a finger to her other ear.

"I can now."

"Right. Well, I was calling because I'm hearing a lot of weird yowling noises from your house. I went to check on your cat, but the door is locked and I won't enter your home without prior notice as your landlord. But the yowling's been going on for about an hour. I don't know where you are, but someone should go check on Sushi soon. The sounds are very... concerning."

"Oh my god, thank you for calling me. I'll be home as soon as I can."

The call ended and Daphne looked around wildly. Bryan was giving the local media a tour of the interior of the building and Kav was directing people to the food trucks and games they had set up. Cade was nowhere to be seen. She had to find him. He was the only one she could pull away today.

She saw another familiar-enough face, though. The physical therapist who had replaced Cade was heading her way. She couldn't remember his name and didn't particularly care for him, but that didn't matter. She could get him to handle the kids' booth while she figured out what was going on at home.

"Hey, you!" Daphne called, pointing to the man she meant. He caught the gesture and joined her.

"How can I help, ma'am?"

Daphne didn't have the energy to be annoyed at being ma'amed. She just told him what she needed, keeping her instructions as simple as possible. He seemed to understand, so she cut a path through the crowd, making her way toward the building with as much speed as she could manage.

When she made it to the large glass windows, she peered through, but she couldn't see Cade anywhere. Cursing internally, she flipped around and started for the food truck area. She made it maybe three steps before she ran into a solid wall of man with a grunt.

"Whoa, you okay there?" She looked up into Cade's laughing eyes, which quickly sobered as he took her in. "What's wrong?"

She filled him in on the call from Tabitha and he handed her his keys. "My car's out back. Go get it. I'll tell Bryan where we're going and meet you where the street's blocked off."

Right. She could do that.

Cade was learning Daphne drove with reckless abandon when Sushi was in danger. He couldn't blame her, especially after how he had lost it when Sushi had escaped the last time.

He could hear the yowling from the car. He wasn't surprised Tabitha had called with concerns. It was like nothing he had ever heard, and it didn't sound pleasant. It sounded like something was wrong.

She unlocked the door with trembling hands, then flung it open. They raced inside, scattering to try and find her. It didn't take long to figure out she was upstairs from the way her yowl was echoing down the staircase.

Daphne beat him up the stairs by a few seconds, dashing into her room to try and find the cat. He took his own, stepping directly into a puddle near his door.

"Daphne, I think she's in here."

At the sound of his voice, and her mother's response,

Sushi let loose another howl that sounded like it was coming from his closet. Which was packed with boxes. Had she gotten underneath one of them and gotten stuck?

He grabbed one and moved it to the bed, over and over until all that was left in the space was his open suitcase. Somehow, it was full of blankets from around the house and what looked like one of Daphne's blouses. Sushi was in the middle of them, but she looked like she was panting and trying to use the bathroom.

"Oh my god, she's giving birth," Daphne said breathily. Cade closed his eyes. Everything made sense now from what he'd read. If she was pushing, that meant a kitten should be coming soon. Well, everything except why she had chosen his suitcase to give birth in when she had a perfectly good nest downstairs, but that was cats for you.

"I'll go get the water and towels. You stay with her."

He got the supplies they'd prepared from Daphne's bathroom and brought them to Daphne, who had sunk to the floor next to the closet door. He set them on the floor in front of her, in case they needed to intervene and help her clean off the kittens.

Cade looked up just in time to see her give birth to the first kitten, wrapped in a gross, gooey membrane. Sushi picked it up and did something with her teeth that looked far more violent than necessary, then cleaned the kitten.

"Wow, the miracle of life is nasty no matter what species you are," he whispered.

"No kidding. That's why I never wanted to have kids," Daphne whispered back. "She seems to be doing pretty well, though."

He settled himself against the other side of the doorway. The cat was now chewing on what Cade guessed was the placenta, and he had to turn away. He and Daphne had done their research and knew that was normal, but god, it was gross. He asked a question, mostly to distract himself.

"Did you come up with names for the kittens? Last time we talked about it, you were still trying to decide on a theme."

Daphne didn't take her eyes off her cat, who looked to be pushing again. "I think I want to stay on the fish theme. Gina said she's likely to have a smaller litter, since she's so small, so we won't have to be too creative. I'll pick the names once I see them, though."

That was good, he thought. They deserved names like their mother, no matter how many there were. Daphne would come up with great names. He had faith in her.

An hour after they'd gotten home, the whole birth process was done and she had two new grandkittens. They were so small—and orange. She hadn't expected that.

"I expected their ears to be floppy, for some reason," Cade said as he watched them nurse.

"That might happen in a few weeks. Who knows? After all, we barely got a glimpse of their daddy. I guess he was orange, though."

A loud knock on the front door startled everyone except the nursing kittens. They didn't seem to have noticed a disturbance.

Daphne rose to her feet, waving at Cade to stay there. "I'll get it and I'll bring food back for mama. She'll need it, and I doubt she'll let them out of her sight to go get it."

She trudged downstairs and opened the door to find Kav standing there with a worried expression on their face.

"Hey, Bry told me Sushi was having some sort of trouble. I wanted to come and check on you, see if you needed anything? I also brought lunch from Noodle Jam, since I figured you wouldn't want to leave her side."

Daphne grinned tiredly at her best friend. That was exactly the kind of thoughtful gesture Kav was famous for. "You missed all the fun. We have grandkittens. Want to come see?"

Their eyes lit up. "Yes!"

She grabbed their hand and led them upstairs. Kav let out a squeal of delight when they saw the babies. "Oh, I just want to snuggle them. I know I can't, but... wow. Just two?"

"Just two. And you can snuggle them in a few weeks once they're a little more sturdy. Any chance you know anybody who wants an orange Scottish Fold baby or two?"

"Oh, I think I know someone very well," they said. Daphne waited for them to continue, but they just watched the cats with an overwhelmed expression.

"Well, who? I need to talk to them."

"You already are. Bryan and I would like to adopt them, if it would be okay with you."

Daphne stared at them. "Really? You want two kittens?"

"Well, we figured they would be happier if they had a friend to play with, right? Especially with as many hours as Bryan and I work sometimes. But we've missed having Sushi around since I moved out, so..."

Daphne grabbed her friend in a crushing hug. "You are gonna be the cutest cat parent ever! I'm so glad we get to keep them in the family."

fifteen

. . .

Cade, Daphne, and Kav were all piled on the floor of Cade's room mere minutes after the clinic closed for the day, when Bryan walked in.

Cade waved up at his boss, who was looking at them with baffled amusement. "Are you comfy?"

"Very," Daphne answered. "Want to join us?"

That made him boom out a laugh. "No, thanks. I actually wanted to borrow Cade for a few minutes, if you can let him up."

Kav and Daphne shifted so they were sitting upright enough that he could slide out from under them.

With a groan, he pushed himself off the floor. Bryan led him back downstairs and out the front door.

Cade's guts churned. Was he about to get fired for leaving early to deal with Sushi? No, that didn't make sense, today had been his last day. It sucked he'd had to leave the party early, but he was a parent and grandparent now. He had responsibilities.

When the door closed, Bryan spoke again, his voice

quiet. "Have you had any luck finding a job since we talked?"

Cade shook his head. "A couple places said I was overqualified, a few others said I was underqualified… you know how it goes."

He nodded. "I didn't want to tell you in case it didn't come through, but…I just got word. I got the grant!"

Bryan's eyes sparkled in the reflected porch light like this was some big achievement, but Cade was confused.

"I have no idea what you're talking about, Bryan. Can you start at the beginning?

"Oh, right." Bryan chuckled. "I applied for a grant that would pay for your salary for the next three years. The job would be a part-time physical therapist and part-time community outreach specialist—so, basically what you were already doing, but more extensive. We want you to go to places all over Clover Hill and the surrounding cities and talk to people about why it's important to take care of your body, and how we can help."

Cade gaped at him. He'd known Bryan was applying for grants, but had never imagined he had been planning all this, let alone that he had applied for a grant specifi-cally so Cade could stay in Clover Hill.

"You want to give me a job? A full-time job that you said you couldn't give me?"

"I said I would see what I could do. There are some requirements for things we have to do in the community, because it is a local grant, but I have a job for you now. And, I already talked to Pop about possibly stealing you, and he's okay with it if you are. There's no one else I'd rather have be the face of my company to the community. If… if you want to be, that is."

Cade didn't have words to answer him with, so he just wrapped him up in a hug as tight as his arms would go.

"I take it that's a yes?" Bryan squeaked. Cade set him back down on the porch, but kept his arm close to steady him.

"Yes!" Cade laughed. "Come on, we've gotta tell Daphne."

The sound of someone sprinting up the stairs startled Daphne out of her reverie.

"What on earth is going on?" Daphne asked breathlessly. "Is everything all right?"

Cade, beaming, ran to her and pulled her to her feet in one smooth motion. "I get to stay! Bryan found funding and I get to stay!"

"What? How?" He twirled her around, laughing like someone who didn't have a single care in the world.

"I got a grant," Bryan explained, filling her in on the details briefly. It was absolutely perfect for Cade. She looked at her partner in dawning realization he didn't have to leave.

The sparkle in his eyes, his hands holding her up by the waist, and the knowledge she wasn't going to lose him led to heat spreading through her body. She wrapped her arms around his shoulders, pulled herself closer and kissed him with all the joy that filled her.

Judging by the way his eyes darkened and the way he held her tight even after he broke the kiss, he was feeling that same heat. She tilted her head toward the bed and he nodded. They didn't need any more communication than that.

"Bryan, I'm sorry to do this so soon after you brought us such great news, but I have to kick you both out. I'm going to make sweet, sweet love to this man I get to keep."

Kav and Bryan laughed in unison, but they didn't argue.

As soon as Bryan was out of the house, Cade scooped her up like a bride and practically ran to the other bedroom. Like the first time they'd made love, their movements were frantic as they stripped off their clothes and tumbled into her bed. Several orgasms later, they lay together in the mess of blankets trying to catch their breath.

She didn't know how long they lay there and she didn't care. She was just enjoying being with him. He was thinking hard about something, though.

"What's on your mind?"

"I was just thinking about how much stuff I'm gonna have to move. You have no idea how many plants I have. Would you be okay with me bringing my aquarium? They're good fish, and I get the feeling Sushi and the kittens would enjoy watching them."

"You said the tank is huge, right? I bet they'd love that. We'll have to make sure they can't get in though. We don't want Sushi to have a sushi dinner."

That made him rumble a laugh. "There will be a lot of details to handle, you know. I think there might be something that would help."

Daphne peered at him. "What's that?"

"A binder. A really big one."

She laughed out loud. He was truly the perfect man for her.

Kitten Caboodle

acknowledgments

This book was a long time in the making, and the product of a lot of love, sweat and tears. But y'all probably don't want to read about that. So here's my big list of thanks for this book.

To my husband, thank you for being yourself and my best partner, all day every day. You're my favorite, always.

To The Broken Circle, for being the best pocket friends I've ever had the opportunity to glitter with. Thank you for reminding me to be my best self, even when that self is weird as hell.

To JR & Skye, for wanting me to be a part of this project even after I missed deadline after deadline and then turned in a book that was 1.5x longer than it should have been.

To Hsinju, Chace, Sasha, and A. Lee, your feedback and friendship has been absolutely invaluable and helped me fall back in love with Kitten Caboodle every time I thought I'd completely lost the plot.

And to my readers, for reminding me that you love my work. I hope I've made your days just a little bit brighter, somehow.

You all helped me make this book into the wonderful novella it is today, and I could not be more grateful.

❀

more by this author

as candace harper

News Flash - FREE for newsletter subscribers

Mrs. Mix Up

Hugs & Quiches

as ceillie simkiss

The Learning Curves Universe:

Learning Curves (#1)

The Ghosts of Halloween (#1.5)

Wrapped Up In You (#2)

The Learning Curves Omnibus (all three above PLUS two brand
new short stories!)

Elisade Universe

An Unexpected Invitation (#0.5)

A Knight to Remember (#1)

Pack Ties (#1.5)

Other:

Second Wind

about the author

Candace Harper is a queer, neurodivergent woman living with her spouse, two cats and a dog in the South. She's known for being overly enthusiastic about silly things and as the "mom friend."

She writes queer fiction as much and in as many genres as she can manage, both under this name and as Ceillie Simkiss. When she's not writing, she's crocheting all kinds of awesome things and sometimes selling them at shop.-foxglovefiction.com!

To keep up with her work, the best places to go are her newsletter, twitter and instagram!

Sign up for the newsletter at foxglovefiction.com!

twitter.com/foxglovefiction
facebook.com/candaceharperauthor
instagram.com/foxglovefiction
bookbub.com/candace-harper